He read alou

'"Awarded to the [...] academic standing in the senior school for the year..."' Blake's voice trailed off as he continued to read, then he turned to look at her. 'Abigail Gibson...four years in a row. Well, I certainly have no reason to be overbearing with you, do I?'

Abby flushed. 'I wish you could forget I said that,' she muttered.

'I shall probably get a little more mileage out of that, just for fun...Abby. With all that...' he nodded towards the wooden shield '...I think I might well need it.'

When he smiled, Abby found herself staring at him, their eyes locked together in a mutual regard that held a new tension in it. This was the first time he had given her all his undivided attention in a personal way out of a hospital setting. The effect was devastating.

Rebecca Lang trained to be a State Registered Nurse in Kent, England, where she was born. Her main focus of interest became operating theatre work, and she gained extensive experience in all types of surgery on both sides of the Atlantic. Now living in Toronto, Canada, she is married to a Canadian pathologist, and has three children. When not writing, Rebecca enjoys gardening, reading, theatre, exploring new places, and anything to do with the study of people.

Recent titles by the same author:

LET TOMORROW COME
SURROGATE FATHER

THE PERFECT
TREATMENT

BY
REBECCA LANG

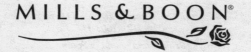

MILLS & BOON®

All the characters in this book have no existence outside the imagination of the author, and have no relation whatsoever to anyone bearing the same name or names. They are not even distantly inspired by any individual known or unknown to the author, and all the incidents are pure invention.

First published in Great Britain 1999
Harlequin Mills & Boon Limited,
Eton House, 18-24 Paradise Road, Richmond, Surrey TW9 1SR

© Rebecca Lang 1999

ISBN 0 263 81892 6

Set in Times Roman 10½ on 11¼ pt.
03-9912-57603-D

Printed and bound in Spain
by Litografia Rosés S.A., Barcelona

CHAPTER ONE

ABBY GIBSON, MD, was late for the general medical rounds at University Hospital, Gresham, Ontario. Her hair was still damp from the shower she had taken about twenty minutes earlier in the hospital medical residence; its dark tendrils clung wetly to her neck.

'Morning, Dr Gibson. You in a hurry as usual?' One of the other occupants of the crowded elevator, a male physiotherapist whom she knew reasonably well, grinned at her as they were crushed inelegantly together against a wall of the moving compartment. In the hospital this was one of the general meeting places of quick hellos and goodbyes.

'Oh…hi, there, Ray!' Abby said breathlessly. 'Yeah, you could say that!' While craning to look at her wristwatch, she dropped two heavy textbooks and a sheaf of papers that she was carrying.

'More haste, less speed!' Her companion grinned again as he eased himself down towards the floor gallantly to pick up her lost items.

'Thanks,' Abby said, taking the books from him. 'How are you, Ray?'

'Chugging along,' he said. 'Living from week to week, like everybody else.'

Abby sighed, conscious of the general atmosphere of stress that prevailed in the hospital these days like an almost tangible cloud; it was a cloud of uncertainty about jobs and teaching positions in a time of severe budget cuts.

'Ray, do you know anything about the new head of the department of internal medicine?' she asked. 'It's his rounds I'm going to be late for.'

'Dr Contini? Mmm, met him a couple of times. Seems

5

like a nice guy. A little young for the job, I would say…if he gets it. You know what this place is like for rumor. Every job has about two hundred applicants. Even at his level, I should imagine.'

'I do know, Ray. Even so, I don't want to be too late for this meeting. First impressions are important, aren't they, if often wrong?' She ran a hand through her damp hair. 'Maybe he won't notice me in the crowd…or my absence.'

'Any red-blooded male would notice you in a crowd, Abby. Slept in?'

'Yes. Crazy week. You're very gallant this morning, Ray.'

'I'm always gallant.'

Abby smiled warmly, though she was preoccupied with the meeting ahead. It was always more than a little nerve-racking meeting a new senior colleague who was in a position to judge you, give you professional evaluations. 'Let's hope the new guy will be, too,' she said.

She did not want to give Dr Contini a negative first impression of her, if she could help it, as they were probably destined to spend a fair amount of time together professionally.

The old chief of the internal medicine department was away on an extended professional trip, she knew that. This new guy, Dr Blake Contini, who was taking his place during his absence, was slated to become the new head of the department when the chief retired, according to rumor.

'See you, Abby. This is where I get off.'

'Bye, Ray.'

The elevator emptied, leaving her the sole occupant.

As she came out moments later at basement level into the corridor that would take her from the east wing to the west wing of the hospital, she put her attaché case and books on the floor and took out her neatly laundered white lab coat to put on over her blouse and skirt.

She strode along the corridor purposefully, trying to look

businesslike even though there was no one else there to see her. Down here, the vista was bleak—utilitarian, empty corridors with garish fluorescent lights.

Up ahead, just where the corridor began a slight incline, Abby could see that someone had dumped a bag of laundry, or something, on the floor. That was part of the problem around here, she thought, not enough maintenance staff now to keep the place clean and tidy, so many laid off.

Coming closer, she could see that the 'bag of laundry' was a person in a lab coat and white pants, slumped awkwardly against the wall. 'Oh, hell!' she said out loud.

It was a man, a middle-aged man with thinning grey hair and a pale, gaunt face—obviously one of the medical staff. Quickly Abby knelt down on one knee beside the recumbent figure, dumping her books and bag in one quick movement. As she heaved the man over onto his back so that she could see his face more clearly, he looked familiar. The lips had a bluish tinge; the eyes were half open, unseeing.

'Mo!' Abby said softly, recognising Dr Will Ryles, the chief of Radiology.

Automatically she felt for the carotid artery at the side of the neck and searched for a pulse, holding her own breath as she did so. Yes, there it was—the faint fluttering of a pulse, rapid, irregular.

'Thank God,' she said, shifting her position so that she was kneeling beside Will Ryles. 'Not a cardiac arrest.'

With steady hands she unbuttoned his shirt and loosened his tie, then listened to his chest with her stethoscope, working quickly. After hastily dragging the necessary equipment from her bag, she took his blood pressure. The systolic blood pressure was only ninety. There was little doubt that he had suffered a myocardial infarct, a heart attack.

Abby looked around frantically. Where were other people when you really needed them? She had to get him to the emergency department at once before he sustained brain damage from low blood pressure—get him on oxygen, have cardiac enzyme tests done and get him on the life-saving, clot-dissolving drugs.

Compassion filled her as she looked down at the man's face which was now an unhealthy yellowish colour and cyanosed from lack of oxygen. He looked exhausted. No doubt he was, she speculated. Beside him on the floor was a cellular telephone, plus a few other items which had obviously fallen out of his pockets. Maybe he had been trying to call for help.

Quickly Abby punched in the number of the emergency department triage station, not knowing whether the phone would function here in the basement. Thankfully, she heard it ringing. Most of the nurses knew her there—she had been there frequently as a medical student and had been one of the last young doctors to do a general training internship before the system had finally been abolished in favour of a new system of early specialization.

'Hi,' she said, when a nurse answered. 'This is Dr Abby Gibson. I've just found Dr Will Ryles, the radiologist, collapsed in the east-to-west wing basement corridor. It's a probable myocardial infarct. He needs oxygen pretty quickly. I need a couple of people here fast with a stretcher. He'll have to be lifted.'

'Right,' the nurse said. 'I'll send a doctor and a nurse right away, with a couple of porters.'

'Thanks.' Abby disconnected the line. 'Dr Ryles! Dr Ryles!' She slapped his face gently, then slightly harder. 'Open your eyes.' Again she placed her fingers over his carotid artery, searching for the faint pulse that would indicate he was alive.

The man moaned, his eyes opening feebly. His expression was blank as he tried to focus on Abby's face while she bent close to him.

'Take it easy,' she said, 'you're ok. You're lying on the floor. You fell down, but you're ok, sir. Just stay where you are, don't try to move. Help is on the way. I'm Dr Gibson.'

Dr Ryles moaned again, letting out his breath on a long sigh and closing his eyes wearily.

'Have you got much pain?' Abby asked, putting her mouth close to his ear and keeping her fingers on his pulse. Poor devil, she thought, feeling her throat close up with emotion. She liked Will Ryles very much; in all his dealings with her he had been unfailingly courteous, very professional, superb at his job, good as a teacher.

He shook his head slightly, mouthed the word 'Ok.'

As she looked at him, Abby also felt anger and frustration. She knew that his department was one of those that was being downsized, so she had heard. New computer technology was enabling X-rays to be read and diagnoses to be made off-site, away from the hospital where the X-rays were taken and the diagnostic procedures done. Businessmen were making decisions about how things should be done, rather than medical professionals, often making vital and important decisions on things they knew little or nothing about.

'Hurry…please, hurry!' Abby whispered the words to herself, looking expectantly down the corridor, praying that the emergency department staff would get a move on.

When she heard the elevator doors opening in the distance and the banging of a stretcher being hastily pushed out, she stood up and gathered up all the bits and pieces of personal belongings that had fallen out of Dr Ryles's pockets. She shoved them into her attaché case to make sure that they didn't get lost in the dash to the emergency department; she would get them to him later, or to his family.

It was Dr Marcus Blair, Head of the emergency department, a nurse and two porters who came hurrying towards her as she turned to greet them. In moments they had an oxygen mask, attached to the portable cylinder, on Will Ryles's face.

'I found him like this a few minutes ago,' Abby explained to Dr Blair. 'He has a pulse, he's conscious. Breathing ok. Blood pressure ninety.'

Dr Blair nodded. 'Right. Let's get him onto the stretcher.'

With all of them helping, they rolled Will Ryles onto a canvas sheet with poles attached, then lifted him onto the wheeled stretcher. Dr Blair put a rubber tourniquet round their patient's arm, preparatory to taking blood samples— he would do that in the elevator as they were going up to the emergency department on the main floor level. They would need blood for the cardiac enzyme tests, electrolyte levels and a hemoglobin test.

'We've got someone holding the elevator for us,' Dr Blair said. 'Come on.'

'Do you need me, Dr Blair?' Abby asked.

'No, we can manage now. Thanks, Dr Gibson. A good thing you came along. It's like the Sahara desert down here.' With that, they set off at a quick trot down the corridor. Abby stood to watch them until she heard the elevator doors close and the elevator move upwards. Only then did she realize how tense she was, like the proverbial bowstring.

'Phew!' She let out a breath she had been holding. 'Thank God for that.'

If anything had happened to Will Ryles she would have felt personally responsible. She could have called a code— the cardiac arrest code, she supposed now—but really he hadn't had a cardiac arrest. He would be all right now.

She felt drained, as though she had already done half a day's work, as well as shaken up by this sad encounter with someone she knew fairly well as a colleague. Someone would now have the unpleasant task of calling his wife to let her know.

'Not a good way to start the morning,' she muttered to herself as she resumed her journey. There was no point now in rushing to the rounds—a good part of the first presentation would be over.

Usually two or three of the residents-in-training, young doctors, presented interesting cases to the department of medicine and anyone else who cared to attend the rounds for learning or interest purposes. As a trainee, she was expected to attend. Sometimes there were photographic slides to look at, sometimes microscopic slides as well if the patient had had a surgical biopsy or other lab work.

Perhaps she could just slip in unnoticed to the small lecture theatre where the rounds were being held this time. If not, she would just have to apologize to Dr Contini, who was running the rounds, and explain the delay.

No such luck, Abby thought resignedly as she entered the room just as one of the window blinds was being let up so that brilliant spring sunshine entered the room at the same time, as though to highlight her late appearance. A slide presentation was obviously just over, indicating that the first case had already been presented. There would probably be one or two more.

Quite a lot of people were present, juniors and seniors alike. Some turned to look at her as she came in. She moved to the back of the room to try to blend in with the small crowd around the coffee urn that was set up on a table.

Moments later she was sipping hot coffee thankfully, holding her bag and books awkwardly with one arm, her mind soberly on Will Ryles. By now they would have the life-saving drugs dripping into his veins via an intravenous line. Would he be relieved, knowing he was out of it for a while, out of the workforce, even though he had a serious condition? Or would he constantly fret about the work he was missing? He was probably one of those guys who pushed himself too hard, not wanting to admit that he needed a break.

Several of her close colleagues were there, those who

were in the same training program, and she made her way towards them. It was then that a firm hand grasped her arm from behind, halting her progress.

'Dr Abigail Gibson, I presume?' a masculine voice said. It wasn't, it seemed to her, a warm voice. It held a sardonic note, a note of censure, and Abby cringed inwardly as she turned to look at the owner of the voice.

As she turned, the heavy books once again slipped from her grasp and landed with a thump at the feet of the speaker, partly covering his shoes. Then, as she stared down at them, a few splatters of coffee from the Styrofoam cup she was holding dotted the cover of the uppermost book.

Feeling clumsy and disconcerted, her mind elsewhere, she found herself stammering. 'Y-yes, I'm Dr Gibson,' she confirmed, raising her eyes to the man who stood looking down at her.

With a sense of shock she looked into cool blue eyes, intelligent eyes that were regarding her with undisguised perceptiveness and not a little exasperation, tinged with surprise...perhaps from the weight of the books on his toes? Abby swallowed convulsively.

'S-sorry,' she added.

He had an attractive, very masculine face, with a fine chiselled bone structure. Instantly she thought of a racehorse, a thoroughbred, with its fine aristocratic frame, perfectly formed for its function. The face was not smiling.

So this must be Dr Blake Contini. Abby felt slightly breathless, rather as though she had been punched in the solar plexus, not least because he was now frowning at her in a way that did not seem justified by her lateness or by the fact that she was a junior doctor in a training position or by the weight on his feet. After all, she was not even in his department as such. It brought an odd feeling, this astute appraisal, coming as it did on top of a sense of mourning that she had for the plight of Will Ryles.

'Sorry,' she muttered again, unable to think of anything else. As she bent carefully at the knees to retrieve her books, a few more drops of coffee escaped from her cup.

'Let me do it, Dr Gibson,' he said, putting out a restraining hand. Abby flushed, feeling as though the entire room had gone silent, that she was the focus of attention. Keeping her gaze lowered, she watched his lean hands wipe the coffee off her books with a handkerchief and pick them up.

'Here,' he said, thrusting the books at her and helping her to tuck them under her arm. 'Better get yourself another cup of coffee.'

'Th-thanks.' For a couple of seconds she thought she detected a touch of humour in his eyes as he looked at her when their hands touched warmly for a moment.

He took a sheet of paper, a computer printout, from the pocket of his lab coat, holding it so that she could see it. For a few seconds she gazed at it blankly.

'This is the summary of the first case we've reviewed today, which you've managed to miss entirely,' he said. 'We're about to start on the second case.' He tucked the paper between the pages of one of her books. Abruptly he turned away.

'Wait a minute,' she said, recovering something of her habitual confidence and composure. 'And you are? I didn't get your name.' He hadn't given his name—that had been a bit boorish, she considered belatedly.

It was almost certain that he was who she supposed him to be, as he had been avidly described to her by several of her women co-workers, yet he could not make the assumption that she would automatically know who he was. The thought of such an assumption fuelled niggles of annoyance.

He turned back to her slowly, an expression of muted surprise on his face. Fixing her with a look that might have quelled a lesser mortal, he held out a hand to her. With his other hand he deftly plucked the coffee-cup from her.

'Don't want any more accidents, do we?' he said sardonically, while Abby was only too aware that other people nearby were staring at them curiously. 'I'm Dr Contini,' he added dryly, gripping her vacant hand firmly. 'Blake Contini—Acting Head of the department of internal medicine.'

'Oh…I see,' Abby said thoughtfully, as though she had had no idea. 'That explains it.'

'I'll talk to you at the end of the session, Dr Gibson. Wait for me,' Blake Contini said, turning away from her.

'Yes, Dr Contini.'

When Abby caught sight of her colleagues in the family practice program looking at her commiseratingly, grinning, she felt her face flush anew. That guy was something else! As soon as these rounds were over she would give him a piece of her mind if he was high-handed with her when she explained about Dr Ryles. As it was, he hadn't even given her an opening to apologize out of politeness. Some of the other staff men would have turned a blind eye to her lateness. Maybe because some of them didn't care, she had to admit in all honesty. Some were good teachers, some were mediocre, some were downright bad.

'What was that all about?' Her colleague and friend Cheryl Clinton approached her. 'Was he mad at you for missing the case?'

'Yeah, I guess so.' Abby shrugged. 'What a high-handed guy. And what a nerve, in front of the whole room.'

'I wouldn't mind getting that sort of attention from him,' Cheryl said, her eyes searching the room for the object of their discussion.

'At least he's got a firm handshake.' Abby tried to laugh it off. 'I can't stand guys whose hands feel like a slab of cheese or the proverbial dead fish. He wants to see me after… I can't wait to give him an earful.'

Cheryl laughed. 'Attagirl!' she said delightedly. 'Put him

in his place.' Then she added, *sotto voce*, 'Pretty dishy, though, eh?'

Cheryl's head turned again towards the tall figure who was now across the room talking to the medical residents who had presented the case Abby had just missed.

'Mmm,' Abby said absently as she turned to follow Cheryl's line of vision, looking at the aquiline profile of Dr Contini. Her thoughts were returning sharply to Dr Will Ryles, wondering what was going on right now with him in the emergency department, whether the staff had informed his wife yet, whether she was at this very moment driving to the hospital with a terrible fear in her heart of what she might find there. As soon as possible she would get down there herself and find out.

'I'm sorry I missed the first case,' she murmured. 'Something happened. I'll tell you about it later, Cheryl.'

The next case was about to be presented. Maybe by the time she got out of this room Dr Ryles would have already been transferred to the coronary care unit.

Dr Contini, as though sensing her eyes on him, turned sharply to look at her over the heads of his new colleagues. His eyebrows rose slightly, questioningly, as their eyes met. Probably, he didn't even know Will Ryles, she told herself angrily.

Refusing to be the first to look away, Abby held his gaze. There was no way that she was going to be intimidated by him. For the second time in the space of a few minutes she felt a sense of shock, a sudden unwelcome stab of acute sexual attraction. Then all attention was focused on two young residents who stood up at the front of the room to present the second case of the rounds.

When the rounds were finally over and the others had gone, Abby lingered in the room, waiting. All the others had left abruptly, having to resume their normal working day. She watched as Dr Contini walked over to the door and closed it, shutting out the sounds of chatter from the retreating staff.

'Well, Dr Gibson,' he said, coming over to her, 'why were you late? And am I right that you're in the second year of the family practice training program?'

'Yes,' she confirmed, looking at him but trying not to stare. 'I've just started the second year.'

Blake Contini had thick, dark hair, cut fairly short, which contrasted dramatically with a pale skin that had only a very faint tan. From a winter holiday, perhaps? Although Abby was quite tall herself, five feet eight inches, he was considerably taller, forcing her to look up at him as she stood there in her sensible flat shoes.

'Are you planning to work as a general practitioner when you've finished training?' he asked, not waiting for her to answer his other question.

'Of course, Dr Contini,' she said, surprised. 'Why else would I be doing it?'

'Plenty of young women doctors get married shortly after training,' he said dryly, 'and don't actually do much practice.'

'Not me,' she said. She managed to keep her tone from sounding rude, although she didn't like his attitude. She had come to these rounds prepared to like and accept him. Now she felt herself to be uncomfortably on the defensive, a feeling which was reasonably alien to her. Yet at the same time she had an instinctive feeling that he had made that remark to find out if she were married. Don't be ridiculous, she told herself fiercely. What's the matter with you? Usually her internal dialogue was not as intense as this...He must be getting to her. Or she was getting broody...or something.

Maybe he, too, was one of the new breed, Abby thought, with a surge of bitterness as the image of Dr Ryles's exhausted features came even more vividly into her consciousness. Maybe he was one of the slash-and-burn brigade who got rid of people without any human considerations, treating them like items in statistical tables.

'I expect residents to be here on time, Dr Gibson,' he was going on. 'Even the family practice residents. I trust that is not too much to ask?' he continued.

'Um…no…of course not. I have a good reason for being late.' And she was getting cynical, too.

'Great,' he said. 'Er…Dr Gibson, are you really with me? I have a distinct impression that you're operating on another plane.'

Blake Contini was aware that he was staring, but couldn't help himself. The girl in front of him—she seemed like a girl to him—had thick, dark chestnut brown hair with bronze highlights and a slight curl to it all over. Little wisps of hair clung attractively to her creamy neck. He had an absurd desire to touch that neck, to breathe in the scent of her hair…

He also recognized the veiled sarcasm in his own voice. That seemed to have become habitual with him these days when he met attractive women—intelligent, capable, womanly women, who were not afraid of their own femininity—who might pose some sort of threat to his outward calm.

Kaitlin had been like that once. Her unwelcome image floated before his mind's eye—blonde, pale, like an ice-maiden now. With the image came the familiar sharp regret…

He disliked himself for his sarcasm as it represented him as something he was not. It reminded him of his own need. Yet it was a useful defense. He knew instinctively that Abigail Gibson was not a man-hater.

Several rejoinders came to Abby's mind, but she bit them back. 'Let me explain,' she said. With few words, she described what had taken place after she had found Dr Ryles collapsed in the corridor, ending with, 'Since you're new here, you may not know Dr Ryles.'

'On the contrary,' he said, his face suddenly stiff with

concern and shock, 'I know him well. I knew him before I came here to University Hospital. Have you checked up on how he is?'

'No, of course not. I came straight here.' And you've been harassing me ever since, she wanted to add.

'Poor old Will.' He murmured the words, as though to himself. 'And an unfortunate experience for you first thing in the morning.' To her surprise, he reached forward to touch her arm commiseratingly. 'You probably saved his life.'

'People *were* rather scarce.'

'I might have known something like this would happen,' he added thoughtfully. 'He's been under so much stress lately, and he pushes himself much too hard.'

'He looked so exhausted when I found him,' she agreed, 'I felt so desperately sorry for him.'

'Yes, he would be exhausted,' Dr Contini said softly, almost as though he had predicted that Dr Ryles would have a heart attack, making Abby speculate on whether they were actually close friends.

'What do you mean?' she asked, picking up nuances. 'Were you, perhaps, aware that he was ill, that he might have an infarct?'

'No…' he said, almost absently, 'Not that. He's been under a lot of strain.'

Blake Contini regretted his sarcasm even more. The eyes that looked back at him frankly were green, large and expressive in a heart-shaped face; there was none of the calculation that he so frequently saw in the expressions of many women he met for the first time.

Across her pert nose, almost classic-shaped, was a faint band of freckles that spilled over onto her cheeks, giving her a mischievous look, rather like a female Huckleberry Finn…one of his boyhood heroes, who now seemed very far away. He found his eyes moving automatically to her mouth, to her lips that were full, beautifully shaped, soft-looking. The impression of her, of softness, produced a sense of dissonance, imposed, as it was, on his acute concern about Will Ryles.

'Um…the first case, the one that I missed,' Abby said, looking at the computer printout he had given her, now feeling the pressure of time. 'I'm sorry about that. I would like to catch up—'

'The patient is on 2 East, so maybe you can get to see him today. I shall be seeing him myself at about eleven o'clock—maybe you can manage to meet me there, Dr Gibson,' he said. 'I can go over a few things with you. I may want to test your group on this particular case later in the year.'

'Thank you. I would appreciate that,' she said formally. 'General practice isn't exactly easy, Dr Contini, even though you specialists might think so. We've got to be good at everything, not just one thing. And keep up to date on it all.'

'I didn't say it was easy, neither do I think so,' he countered. If he was surprised by her remarks, he hid it well.

'Start as you mean to go on,' her mother had always told her. While she understood that to be an aphorism generally referring to marriage, it was, she considered, a good bit of advice to keep in mind at the start of any relationship.

'I'll try to get there,' Abby said stiffly, very conscious suddenly that they were alone in the room, that she was inappropriately attracted to him. 'I am expected at a family practice clinic right now—Dr Wharton's clinic in Outpatients.'

'I'm going to Outpatients myself. I'll call Dr Wharton and arrange for you to have time off at eleven o'clock,' he said. Then, making up his mind about something, he looked at his watch with a quick flick of the wrist. 'If you would like to see Dr Ryles as much as I would, I can call the outpatient clinic, tell them you're going to be late, then we could visit him briefly in the coronary care unit.'

Abby nodded. 'Yes. Thank you. I would like to see him, find out what's happened.'

'Sorry about my obtuseness earlier.' He had the grace to apologize. 'I had, of course, no idea.'

'No,' Abby said quietly, managing to imply by her tone that one should not make flash judgements. He was very attractive, she acknowledged again, lowering her eyes to the paper she held. There was even a hint that he would, perhaps, have a natural charm if he were to let himself go a bit. Not that she was one to talk...

'I'll see if I can set it up,' he said, 'and find out where Dr Ryles is.'

'I hope he's survived,' she ventured.

'So do I.'

As he strode over to a telephone in the room she watched him, her mind active. His reaction to her news, for someone new to the hospital, had been greater than she had expected. She wondered where he would have met Dr Ryles, who had been at University Hospital for at least twenty-five years.

All at once, she had a very odd, very powerful premonition that Dr Contini would figure large in her life...and not just on the professional level. The feeling was so strong, so peculiar, that she shivered. Telling herself that she was being ridiculous, she turned away from him to stare out the window, away from his disturbing presence.

It wouldn't do for her to feel anything of that nature for her senior colleague. She had made a pact with herself not to get involved with anyone before she had at least finished her post-graduate training and got herself established in her first permanent job as an MD. There was no time for real romance; she had to earn a living, had to give something back to her parents who had supported her so unselfishly all her life, among other things helping to meet the financially crippling fees for medical school. They were going to need it. Her dad often joked that if they could remain the working poor, rather than the non-working poor, they would be all right. She seldom forgot that 'joke' for long.

Not that she would be Dr Contini's type. She frowned down at the paper in her hand, the words a blur. Probably he would go for a high-society woman. Anyway, she found herself speculating, he would no doubt be married—he must be in his mid-thirties.

Maybe she found him disturbing because he reminded her of what she had never had…real love, passion. Maybe that was it, when such a large part of her own life was, through necessity, focused on work. At the same time, she felt a certainty that he could be a formidable enemy.

She walked to the door to wait for him, all at once wanting to get out.

'I spoke to the emergency department,' he said, coming over to join her. 'He's in the coronary care unit now. Still all right.'

'That's great,' she breathed, relieved of a sense of responsibility.

They collided as he moved to open the door for her and she moved to open it for herself. 'Steady,' he said, smiling. 'Tell me, Dr Gibson, are you usually this…er…'

'Klutzy?' she offered.

The smile on his face broadened slowly, lightening his attractive features, ironing out subtle signs of strain. Abby found herself transfixed, staring at him at close quarters, as he held his arm in front of her to secure the heavy door. With his face only inches from her own, she had the absurd urge to lean forward and place her lips against his firm mouth.

'That isn't the word I would have used,' he quipped, 'but it's as good as any, I guess. I don't mean to be unkind.' He added the last words softly, in such a way that Abby felt as though she were melting, leaning towards him. Don't be ridiculous, she told herself yet again…

'I am frequently this way,' she conceded, forcing a jokey

tone. 'My friends tell me it's a sign of genius, the absent-minded-professor syndrome, so naturally I take them at their word.'

'Hmm…let's hope they're right. Such a trait could be a professional liability.' Still he smiled, his eyes exploring her face.

'Oh, they are right!' she insisted, pushing past him to get out, aware of him physically with every sense in her being.

'Just to be on the safe side, Dr Gibson, let me carry those books,' he said.

CHAPTER TWO

THE coronary care unit was quiet, peaceful, set up in an area of the acute-care floor of the hospital where there was no through traffic and where noise could be kept to a bare minimum. They entered through a heavy door that closed silently behind them.

A nurse sat at a desk in the nursing station, looking at a bank of individual computer screens which were monitoring the four patients who were in her section. Each patient was connected up to leads going to the electronic equipment which would relay the information to the screen. Any irregularities of heartbeat, blood pressure and oxygen levels of the blood would immediately be known.

Although all was peaceful, Abby knew that she would not want to be a patient here, lying in bed, wondering if your heart would stop at any moment. Walking beside Dr Contini, she looked around her as they approached the nurse silently.

'Is Dr Ryles here?' he asked. The nurse gestured towards an area down a short corridor where there were a few individual rooms.

'Room three,' she said with a smile.

'How is he?' Abby said.

'Pretty good, considering. He's stable now. His wife's with him at the moment,' the nurse said. 'He's sleeping, so we don't really want him to be disturbed.'

'Sure,' Dr Contini said. 'We won't wake him.'

In room three, Dr Ryles lay on his back in the narrow bed, the monitor leads attached to his bare chest. A small computer screen by the bed showed the spiky graph of his heartbeat, as well as the heart rate and blood pressure.

Abby's eyes went automatically to that screen as they entered silently. What she saw there confirmed that he was stable, his blood pressure near normal, the heartbeat good.

He was still on oxygen, his colour good now, while intravenous fluids dripped slowly from a litre plastic bag hung beside the bed. Abby felt her anxiety diminish somewhat. The team from the emergency department had been in time after all.

Mrs Ryles, who looked about the same age as her husband, was sitting beside the bed, her face turned to him. She rose to her feet as they stopped at her side. Her pale face showed evidence of tears, the eyelids swollen and red, and she registered surprised pleasure at seeing Dr Contini.

'Hello, Ginny,' he said softly, holding out his arms to her. 'I'm sorry to be meeting you again so soon under these circumstances.'

'Oh, Blake.' The woman's voice trembled as she went gratefully into the arms that Dr Contini offered her. They embraced in a silent hug. 'Thank God you're here.'

So they were friends after all. Abby stood aside, watching them, her own emotions very close to the surface as she saw the tears again on the wife's face. When they had satisfied themselves that Dr Ryles was indeed all right, Dr Contini gestured that they should go outside to the main corridor where they could talk without disturbing anyone.

'This is Dr Gibson,' Blake Contini introduced her when they were outside. 'She was the one who found Will.'

Mrs Ryles grasped Abby's outstretched hand with both her own. 'I want to thank you,' she said, her voice trembling. 'I understand that he was in the basement, where he might not have been found for some time. If you hadn't found him... hadn't known what to do, or what you were looking at...he might not have survived. Thank you. You saved his life.'

'I—I'm very glad that I was there,' Abby said. 'I...really didn't do a lot. I was just able to call someone.'

'You were there—that's the main thing!' Ginny Ryles said emphatically. 'It's all this business about the downsizing that's going on here, you know, that has brought this on with Will…all the budget cuts.'

'That's most likely a contributing factor,' Abby agreed wryly, as the distraught woman articulated more or less what she had been thinking herself that morning.

'It's all the underhand business of deliberately running down departments, without telling the professional staff what has been planned, so that private companies can take over the radiology work of this hospital,' Ginny Ryles went on with bitter passion, as though she had been waiting to speak to someone about it for a long time.

Abby nodded, while Dr Contini stood silent. 'I don't doubt that for one moment…not for one moment,' Mrs Ryles went on. 'He's talked about nothing else for weeks. All the stress… It has to get to someone. It has to.'

'Yes,' Abby agreed, picking up the frustration in the woman's words.

Blake Contini took the woman's arm. 'Come with me to the hospital cafeteria, Ginny,' he said kindly. 'I'll buy you coffee, or anything you want. We can talk there. Dr Gibson has to get to Outpatients.'

'Thank you, Blake. You're very kind, and I do appreciate it,' Ginny Ryles said.

'Dr Gibson.' Blake Contini turned to Abby. 'I'll see you in Outpatients in a little while. I have some patients to see there. I'll square things for you with Dr Wharton about taking time off.'

'All right. Thank you,' Abby said. 'Well, goodbye, Mrs Ryles. I expect I'll see you again, I'll probably look in later… He's in good hands.'

'Thank you again, Dr Gibson. I'm planning to spend most of the day here with Will. I'll only go out of my mind if I stay at home,' Mrs Ryles said quietly.

'There's every indication that he's going to be all right,'

Dr Contini reassured her gently, while Abby looked at him surreptitiously with new eyes.

Yes, it was clear that he could be charming. She wondered momentarily what it would be like to be the object of that charm, that warmth and undivided attention. Perversely, uncharacteristically, she found herself longing for it—almost as though the incident with Will Ryles had jolted her out of a deep sleep, like Sleeping Beauty in the fairy-tale—then brought her face to face with the prince. Snap out of it, Abigail Gibson, she admonished herself once again. Get real!

'Thank you for saying that,' Mrs Ryles said tremulously, trying to inject some hope into her voice. 'Here I am, going on about our affairs, but what about you, Blake? How's Kaitlin? Any change there?'

'No, nothing,' Dr Contini said heavily.

'Is there likely to be?'

'I doubt it very much.'

As Abby made her way to Outpatients a little later, she puzzled over that last brief verbal exchange. It was evident that Dr Contini had known Dr Ryles and his wife for quite a long time.

She sighed, looking at her wristwatch and making an effort to shift her thoughts to the work ahead in the clinic. She was looking forward to it.

It was only too easy to become obsessional about the internal politics of a hospital, which were so closely connected to the broader political scene. It could sap one's energy. Although it was of concern to her, as much as she knew that one had to get involved in some degree, she did not have time for that right now.

Who, she wondered, was Kaitlin? The question nagged at her persistently...as did the tone of Blake Contini's voice when he had replied, 'No, nothing.'

The voice had sounded dead, devoid of all emotion.

Dr Wharton's clinic was well under way when she got

to Outpatients. The young family practice doctors like herself were given new patients to see so that they could take detailed histories, do extensive physical examinations, order blood tests, urine tests, X-rays if necessary, and anything else that might be required before the consultant in charge—in this case Dr Wharton—saw each patient to confirm, or call into question, the preliminary diagnosis. This system saved the senior GPs a lot of time, as well as being a good training exercise for the young doctors, who were themselves MDs.

'Morning, Sue' Abby smiled at the receptionist sitting behind the desk off the main waiting room in the family practice unit. 'Sorry I'm late. Anything interesting for me? I have to leave again for a while just before eleven o'clock to see a patient on 2 East, one of Dr Contini's patients that I missed at the rounds. Is he—does he—Dr Contini, that is—have many patients here this morning?'

Although Abby felt her face flushing as she asked the question, and still feeling somewhat disturbed by all that had happened already that morning, it was good to be in the relative peace of the family practice clinic. Abby felt herself beginning to relax, her habitual confidence returning. This was her territory.

'Hi, Dr Gibson.' Sue, the young, efficient receptionist smiled back. 'It's going to be one of those days, I think. Lots of interesting cases for you to get your teeth into. Here's your first.' She handed over a folder that contained the patient's basic statistics and initial complaint. 'Dr Contini has a couple of patients to see. He told me he'd be available for any consultations here if anyone wanted him.'

'That's really great! Maybe I'll take advantage of that offer, if Dr Wharton's busy. Thanks.' Abby took the folder, glancing at it to see the patient's name and feeling an upsurge of anticipation at working in the same unit with Blake Contini, even though it was an anticipation tinged with remnants of irritation.

Dr Wharton would be there in the unit, plus two other family practice MDs in training like herself. At the moment there was no sign of them—no doubt they were already in the offices assigned to them, seeing patients.

'Mr Barlow,' she called out across the waiting room, 'Gary Barlow.'

A thin man, wearing an old raincoat, got up from a chair, nodding to Abby. 'This way, sir,' she said. Leading the way, she proceeded to the small examination room which was to be her office for the duration of the clinic.

'Take your coat off, Mr Barlow. Have a seat there next to the desk. I'm Dr Gibson. I'll be seeing you first—taking a history, doing an examination—then Dr Wharton will see you.'

With the folder open on the desk in front of her, she read the chief complaint that this patient had. 'Chronic bronchitis' it read, followed by a question mark, then 'Persistent chronic cough.' That would have been written by Sue from the patient's own description of what was wrong with him. Many of their patients came there without any reference letter from any other doctor; they simply telephoned the hospital, asking to see a GP. Many had never had a family doctor.

Mr Barlow, in his fifties, was thin and tired-looking, with a drooping face of loose skin that reminded Abby of a bloodhound. The top of his head was bald. In general, he did not look particularly healthy. He sounded slightly breathless from the simple effort of having walked from the waiting room and taken off his coat. He sat down heavily in the chair next to her desk. Abby took some history sheets from the pile on her desk to add to the file, prepared to do a fair amount of writing.

'It says here that you have a chronic cough, Mr Barlow,' she began, her pen poised above the paper, 'Tell me when that first started, and any other symptoms associated with it.'

For the next few minutes she wrote busily while he talked. It seemed to her that he was trying to minimize the length of time he had had the cough, as well as his level of concern about it. He said he had had a cough for about a year, then it had got worse over the winter, showing no signs of going now that spring was here. He was the sort of man, she suspected, who would not go to a doctor for many years, then would only go finally when symptoms were such that he could not ignore them and his level of anxiety got to a point where he could not think of much else.

'And do you smoke, Mr Barlow?' Abby looked up.

'Yes,' he said.

'For how many years have you smoked?' she asked, keeping her voice neutral with no hint of judgement. 'And how many cigarettes a day?'

'Well...' he said, thinking back, 'I reckon I had my first cigarette when I was about fifteen. Now I smoke about forty a day, give or take a few.'

My God! Abby thought, keeping her face impassive as she wrote again. It was difficult to imagine getting through that many in one day, yet some people, she knew, got through more than that. 'For how many years have you smoked forty a day?' she asked, looking at him and watching his pale, watery eyes go blank as he stared across the room, trying to remember back that long.

'Oh...' He hesitated. 'I suppose it must be at least ten years...about that.'

She wrote down the statistics. 'When did you last have a chest X-ray?' she said.

'A chest X-ray?' He looked surprised. 'I've never had one.'

It never ceased to amaze Abby that many people who smoked heavily could tune out all the publicity and the statistics that were everyday knowledge about smoking and lung cancer. It was as though by some mental gyration they could dissociate it all from themselves, almost as though for health purposes they lived on another plane. That ability, if one could call it that, was very common, of course…and not just with smoking and lung cancer. It certainly applied also to hepatitis and AIDS, particularly among the population taking street drugs.

Maybe she shouldn't be surprised, really, as nicotine was a powerful drug of addiction, although it was frequently not thought of as such. It produced a craving from which it was not easy to break free. Again, she was careful not to inject any hint of judgement in her tone. Sometimes patients would get up and leave if there was any hint of negative judgement about their behavior, past and present.

'When did you last see a doctor?'

He hesitated, calculating. 'Not for a long time. Never needed to,' he asserted, with a hint of defiance. 'Must have been about ten years ago, I guess. Had a tooth abscess. Had to have it pulled out. The guy gave me a quick once-over, then sent me to a dentist.'

'I see,' Abby said, writing that down. 'Any other health problems?'

'Nope,' he said.

'What about your general health? Your appetite?' For the next little while she questioned him about the present, then went on to his medical history, starting from as early in his life as he could remember. Apparently he was one of those men who took his bodily functioning, his health, entirely for granted, having only a very rudimentary knowledge of the anatomy and physiology of the human body.

Abby filled in a requisition form for a chest X-ray, to be done that day in the hospital. If she didn't get it done now he might never come back, especially if he got scared— any more scared than he was now. She did not want to give him a hint that he might have lung cancer, the possible diagnosis that was uppermost in her mind. He could also have chronic emphysema, a lung disease brought on by repeated chest infections, as well as by smoking. This disease also affected the heart.

She also filled in requisition forms for some basic blood work, to be done in the hospital labs. Chronic smokers were often anemic, as well as suffering from various vitamin deficiencies, as they were frequently poorly nourished. Smoking tended to dull the appetite and become a substitute for food.

'I want you to have a routine chest X-ray this morning, Mr Barlow,' she said, 'as soon as we've finished seeing you here. I'll call them to fit you in right away.' There was no way she was going to let him get out of the hospital without one. 'And I want to have some blood tests done as well, then we'll see you here two weeks from now with the results.'

'Ok,' he said, a certain bravado in his voice. 'Have I got bronchitis?'

'I'll be better able to answer that question maybe when I've examined you,' she said, 'which I'm going to do right now. I want to listen to your chest, take your blood pressure, and so on. I'd rather wait for the chest X-ray before saying anything definite.'

The lungs did not expand well. Abby listened to the breath sounds in those lungs as she placed her stethoscope here and there on her patient's chest when he was lying on the examination couch a few minutes later. It was probable that he did have a chronic lung disease, bronchitis or emphysema, which did not rule out cancer as well. There was also the possibility of tuberculosis, which was increasing in prevalence these days.

When she had done a very thorough examination, she lifted the telephone to tell the receptionist that she was ready for Dr Wharton to see her patient.

'He's just gone in with one of the other young doctors,' Sue informed her. 'Dr Contini might be free between his cases. Would you like him?'

'Oh…um…yes, if that's all right with Dr Wharton.' Abby felt herself to be a little flustered, not a state to which she was accustomed. Indeed, she prided herself on her *sang froid*.

'Dr Wharton's in full agreement,' Sue said chirpily, giving Abby the impression that the receptionist was coming under the influence of the new head of medicine. 'He's running late, and Dr Contini wants to learn the ropes here.'

While waiting for Dr Contini, Abby called the X-ray department to make an appointment for Gary Barlow, stressing that she needed it done that morning, soon. As a chest X-ray could be done very quickly, they gave her a time which would coincide with the end of Mr Barlow's appointment in Outpatients. Considering that he might leave the hospital without the X-ray she resolved to escort him to the X-ray department herself.

She was also keeping a close eye on the time, mindful of her obligation to go to 2 East.

Dr Contini came in after a peremptory knock. 'What can I do for you, Dr Gibson?' Again he reminded her of a racehorse, lean yet muscular, with a graceful, contained power.

'Would you confirm my physical findings, please, Dr Contini?' she said, handing him her written notes. 'That's what Dr Wharton does. Here's the history.'

She watched his dark head as he bent over her notes on the desk, his arms propping him up as he stood reading intently, yet ready to take flight.

'You take a good history, Dr Gibson,' he said, looking up suddenly.

'Of course,' she said, pursing her lips a little. 'I'm well known for my good histories…among other things. I've pencilled in my provisional diagnosis.' Moving over next to him, she put her finger on what she had written, not wanting to say anything in front of Mr Barlow. Quickly, she moved back, oddly aware as she did so that Blake Contini knew she was distancing herself from him.

With an astute look, he smiled at her slightly—there seemed to be a sadness in that look. Instantly she regretted her pursed mouth, her touch of primness, which wasn't really 'her'. Then that name came to mind again…Kaitlin. Who was she? His wife, perhaps? A child? The words that Mrs Ryles had uttered echoed in her mind. 'Any change there?' the woman had said. His dead voice had answered, 'No, nothing.'

Abby knew then that she did not want him to be married, to be committed. It meant that her own resolve was weakening. And she had another year to go of training. 'I appreciate this,' she said. 'There might be something that I've overlooked.'

'We'll see,' he said, taking a stethoscope from the pocket of his lab coat. 'Hello, Mr Barlow. I'm Dr Contini. I understand you have a chronic cough.'

It was five minutes after eleven o'clock when she arrived breathlessly on 2 East, having managed to escort Mr Barlow to X-Ray, just to make sure he would actually go there, and to see two more patients as well.

'If you're looking for Dr Contini,' a nurse said, 'he's down that way. Room six.' She gestured down the corridor of the general medical floor.

'Thanks.'

'We're keeping that patient, Mr Simmons, in isolation,' the nurse said. 'You'll find the stuff you have to put on in the anteroom.'

There was a small glass panel in the door of room six, through which Abby could see Blake Contini, dressed in a gown, cap and mask, talking to the patient.

Mr Ralph Simmons, a man in his early sixties, had a diagnosis of acute myelogenous leukemia, a disease which left him anemic and generally debilitated and thus more susceptible than normal to infections which he might pick up from other people. Abby put on a gown in the small anteroom, covering her own clothes, then a disposable cap that covered her hair and a face mask. Last, she put on a pair of latex gloves.

'Ah, Dr Gibson,' Dr Contini said, as she let herself into the room, his eyes going over her quickly. 'We've been waiting for you. I've told Mr Simmons to expect you.'

'Good morning.' Ralph Simmons smiled tiredly at Abby.

'Good morning,' she answered, moving to stand near Blake Contini at the bedside. He held the patient's chart.

Mr Simmons lay on the only bed in the room. He was a large man, who had most likely once been very fit and muscular, Abby surmised as she looked at him. He seemed to be still in reasonable shape, although very pale and tired-looking.

'Did you have time to read the computer printout I gave you earlier?' Dr Contini asked.

'Yes, I did.'

'Good. Here's the case-history chart.' He handed it to her so that she could read about their patient in more detail, see the results of the blood tests that had been done so far in order to make the diagnosis and assess the degree of development of the disease. 'Mr Simmons knows his diagnosis.'

He meant, Abby supposed, that they could talk reasonably freely about it in front of the patient.

'How are you feeling, Mr Simmons?' she asked.

'Tired,' he said. 'Very, very tired.'

Before Abby had entered medical school she had been under the impression that it was children who commonly suffered from the various types of leukemia that were known—only later had she discovered that it was just as common in adults, right up to the elderly. In fact, the incidence of the disease peaked in the sixth and seventh decades.

She knew now that the prognosis for anyone over the age of sixty was not as good as for a younger person, mainly because the greater a person's age the less likely they were able physically to tolerate the toxic effects of the very potent chemotherapy treatments that were required to put the disease into remission.

'As I'm sure you know,' Dr Contini said quietly, looking over her shoulder at the open chart, addressing both her and the patient, 'the cause of acute leukemia is unknown, although some links with toxic chemicals have been demonstrated in some cases. We've been discussing possible future treatment, Dr Gibson.'

'I see,' she said.

Mr Simmons nodded his understanding, his eyes on Dr Contini. From before his admission to hospital, he had known the probable diagnosis from his GP, and had insisted on being told the truth. 'I would like to know as much about it as I can,' he said.

'It's a disease characterized by the proliferation of immature blood cells arising in the bone marrow, where blood cells are made,' Abby's colleague continued, addressing Mr Simmons. 'All it takes is the transformation of a single bone marrow cell into a malignant form… From then on, this one cell produces clones of itself, which gradually spread to other parts of the body, especially to the spleen and liver, where they accumulate and cause problems.'

'What sort of time frame are we talking about here?' Mr Simmons asked.

'Well, acute leukemia can develop in three months,' Dr Contini said, while Abby kept her eyes on the chart, 'which seems to be so in your case.'

What he did not say, Abby noted, was that some patients had a preleukemic syndrome, which could last for very much longer than three months. The ultimate outcome for patients who had that syndrome was not as good as for those who developed the acute phase more quickly. From the evidence before them, it seemed that Mr Simmons had had a fairly abrupt onset, if he were not glossing over any earlier symptoms.

'Mmm…that's about right,' their patient murmured. Apparently a very intelligent and perceptive man, he would have a good idea of his chances for recovery.

'He's had a lot of investigations,' Abby commented quietly to Dr Contini as she carried the chart to the end of the bed and stood there, looking through it.

'Yes,' he murmured, having moved to stand beside her, his head close to hers as they looked at the hematology lab reports together. 'As you know, it's a guide in good medicine that when making a diagnosis one should think of the common things first, before going on to the more unusual and to the exotic. Hence all these blood tests.'

'Yes,' she agreed, conscious of his closeness.

'You may know the saying with regard to making a diagnosis—"When you hear the sound of galloping hooves, think of horses, not zebras."'

Abby smiled. 'Yes, I have heard that. And certainly not unicorns,' something prompted her to add.

'No, not unicorns.' He smiled slightly in return. 'Not that leukemia is difficult to diagnose. We have to be sure of the type, though.'

Abby nodded.

Dr Contini turned again to their patient. 'These immature cells—which never develop to full maturity, Mr Simmons—are unable to perform the functions of the mature cells that they gradually replace…thus the symptoms that you experience, especially the anemia,' he said.

'Yes.'

'Because you have fewer and fewer normal red blood cells, with less and less hemoglobin as a result, you gradually become unable to carry as much oxygen on your red blood cells…which is why you get breathless on exertion.'

Their patient nodded. He seemed avid for information,

as though that in itself might help him to fight this vicious disease, if only on a psychological level.

'Mr Simmons has been in here for two days, Dr Gibson, waiting for the results of more blood tests. I'm here today to discuss treatment with him. Any questions you want to ask him?'

'Has a bone-marrow biopsy been done?' she asked.

'Yes,' Dr Contini said. 'That, as you know, is the other diagnostic test, which shows up the abnormal bone marrow cells, the immature forms.'

Although most of the background information was already in the chart, Abby preferred to hear it directly from the patient. He would most likely have a need to talk. 'What were your initial symptoms, Mr Simmons?' she asked, moved by his air of abject exhaustion, his outward calm, she suspected, masking a great deal of underlying apprehension.

'Well…I was pretty tired all the time, much more so, I suspected, than was warranted by my age,' he said, 'although I lead a hectic life. I teach at the university—political science—and this is a busy time, coming up to the end of the academic year. Even so, I suspected that something was wrong with my health.'

'I see,' Abby said kindly, encouraging him to go on.

'Also, my skin was very pale and I got breathless easily on the slightest exertion, whereas before I could walk for miles. I felt unwell for a lot of the time and I got several colds, as well as chest infections, which I couldn't shake off.'

'Do you smoke?'

'No. Never have done.'

'Anything else?'

'I noticed that I bruised easily, and I couldn't remember having injured myself in any way to cause the bruises,' the patient went on. 'Then my dentist noticed that my gums were bleeding more readily than usual, so when I told him my other symptoms he advised me to see my doctor right away. Then when I went to my GP for a check-up he found out I was very anemic… Then things progressed from there.'

'He had some nausea as well, which indicates some involvement of the gastro-intestinal tract—either infection or bleeding, or both,' Dr Contini said quietly.

'I see.' Abby nodded. 'And what is the planned treatment?'

'I'm getting on to that now,' Dr Contini said. 'What I'm going to do, Mr Simmons, is build up your general resistance before we start you on a course of chemotherapy. If you agree, that is. Since you're very anemic, I'm going to give you a blood transfusion of packed cells, plus some fresh plasma which will help the clotting function of your blood, which gets out of whack with this disease.'

'When am I going to get that?' Mr Simmons asked.

'We'll start this afternoon. The hematology lab is getting you cross-matched. When we've done that, we'll discuss the treatment further. If we decide on chemotherapy later, you get a combination of drugs over a period of five to ten days—that's called the "induction therapy".'

'I've read something about that,' Mr Simmons said ruefully. 'It kills off all the abnormal cells. Right? Or almost all? I guess it makes you feel pretty awful, as well as making your hair fall out.'

Blake Contini nodded.

CHAPTER THREE

WHEN the consultation was over and the two doctors were out in the wide corridor again, divested of their protective clothing, Blake Contini drew Abby to one side, out of the way of the pedestrian traffic, and queried her about aspects of the disease.

'How would you make the final diagnosis here, Dr Gibson?' he asked, fixing her with an astute glance from those rather unnerving blue eyes.

Abby cleared her throat, feeling a little like a student taking an exam. At the same time, she was grateful to have this opportunity for learning—even if her feelings towards her teacher were a little mixed. There was no time now to dwell on that.

'Well,' she began, 'there are abnormal cells in the blood and in the bone marrow—tests for those would be decisive. The cells in the bone marrow never mature beyond the myeloblast level.' Abby met his glance squarely, warming to her subject. 'And, of course, the proliferating leukemia cells accumulate in the bone marrow, eventually suppressing the production of normal blood cells and the normal bone-marrow elements.'

'Yes.'

'He would have evidence of abnormal blood-clotting function—an elevated prothrombin time and low fibrinogen levels, as well as the clinical findings,' she added decisively.

'Right.'

Mr Simmons had manifested two common clinical signs. Abby had felt those distinctly when she had examined him as well—an enlarged spleen and an enlarged liver. They

were signs indicative of a blood disease. 'He has hepato-
megaly and splenomegaly,' she said, 'two other diagnostic
signs.'

He nodded. 'Quite right. After the transfusions that we're
going to give him, how would you proceed with treatment,
Dr Gibson?'

'Well…' Abby took a deep breath. 'I would give him
the remission induction chemotherapy that you mentioned—provided we think he's a good candidate. We hope
to induce a complete remission. We would need to really
build him up first, including, probably, the giving of broad
spectrum antibiotics to try to get rid of residual infection,
particularly if he has some gastrointestinal involvement.'

'Yes…good. I can see that you know your stuff Dr
Gibson,' Blake Contini conceded, raising his dark eyebrows
at her and giving her a small smile, a gesture that trans-
formed his lean face.

They had moved well away from the door of room six
to discuss their patient, yet Abby glanced at it, feeling a
familiar sense of pity. 'I expect he was generally a very fit
man before this,' she said. 'He doesn't smoke, has always
exercised regularly.'

'Yes,' he agreed. 'We'll see what the packed cells and
the plasma do for him over the next day or two. I try to be
as hopeful as I can with these patients. After all, what's the
point of trying to play God when each case is somewhat
different from the next. We can only talk in probabilities.
Do you agree?'

'Yes.'

'There's nothing to stop him from getting hold of a medical book, of course, and reading about probabilities for
himself,' he commented dryly.

'No, he's obviously done some reading.'

'Do you think he's a candidate for a bone marrow transplant?' he asked, looking at her quizzically again.

Abby shrugged, indicating her uncertainty. 'Statistically

speaking…I'm not sure,' she said slowly. 'His age is not on his side.' She considered how well Mr Simmons would stand up to the effects of the toxic drugs that would be required prior to a transplant of bone marrow. 'But I…I wouldn't want to rule it out.'

'Quite right, on both counts,' he said crisply, 'so I don't think that's an undisputed option. We'll see. Before we start chemo, we need to do another liver function test and make sure his kidneys are in good working order.'

A small silence ensued, while other staff moved busily past them in both directions.

'Well…' Abby said, thinking of her outpatient clinic yet oddly reluctant to bring this teaching session to an end, 'thank you for the time you've taken to go over this case with me, Dr Contini. I guess I ought to be getting back…'

Dr Contini looked at his wrist watch. 'That's the least I could do since you missed the presentation because of Will Ryles. A quick cup of coffee is in order, I think, don't you?'

'Definitely,' she agreed.

'Come to my office,' he said lightly, 'then I can quiz you about your attitudes and biases, Dr Gibson.' The smile he gave her surprised her once again, as did his almost playful propensity to goad her in a gentle way, just out of the blue. Although he would not suffer fools gladly, she suspected, he would also be quick to burst any bubble of pomposity wherever he found it…and there was certainly plenty of pomposity in a hospital setting. For this reason, she found herself warming to him even more.

As she gave him a quick sideways glance, Abby reconfirmed her convictions about the false veracity of first impressions; she didn't know what to think about Dr Contini. Two things were certain—he was an unusually attractive man, and knowing him was going to be a challenge, both personally and professionally.

'You said you were good at other things, as well as taking histories,' he said. It seemed that he was determined to shake off the slightly sombre mood that had been engendered by Mr Simmons's condition. 'Tell me what some of those other things are.' His hand lightly under her elbow indicated that they should walk and talk at the same time.

'Well...' Enjoying his touch, she walked slowly. 'I'm pretty good in a crisis.' Looking at him sideways again, she challenged him to contradict her, her full lips curving up at the corners in an involuntary smile.

'I expect you are,' he conceded thoughtfully, his voice husky.

'Even though you think I'm a bit klutzy?' Her smile broadened.

'You said that—I didn't,' he reminded her. 'I would have come up with a word that was more complimentary.'

'I'm not sure I believe that,' she said.

As he led the way to a quiet side corridor off the main second-floor corridor, where the department of internal medicine offices were situated, Abby considered, a little nervously, what he might query her about, and she began to think that maybe she should have declined the offer of coffee.

'Dr Wharton will be wondering what's taking me so long,' she ventured, as he led the way into his cosy office.

'I spoke to Dr Wharton. It's all right,' her colleague informed her. 'This is a teaching hospital after all. You haven't told me what else you're good at...outside work. I like to know who—and what—I'm dealing with in my new colleagues.'

'Well...' Abby racked her brains. 'I'm good at gardening, and I make a pretty mean rum baba when I'm in the mood for it.'

Although she had not intended to make him laugh, his uninhibited amusement at her response was very gratifying.

'Perhaps you'll let me experience that some time,' he said, still grinning. 'I shall look forward to it. Coffee?'

'Please. I'm desperate for coffee and was beginning to

think you weren't going to give me any after all.' Trying to cover up overt signs of her growing attraction to him, she pushed her unruly hair away from her forehead and fussed around with her attaché case which she placed on his desk.

'A coffee now in exchange for a rum baba at a date yet to be decided. Right?' The tone was light.

'Right,' she said unthinkingly, aware only that her heart was beating faster than normal and that she wanted more than anything to be able to meet him outside a work setting—not thinking beyond that.

'Back to serious things. Tell me about your personal ethics, Dr Gibson,' he said, as he handed her a cup of coffee. 'Would you like to sit—get more comfortable?'

'I...I prefer to stand,' she said.

'So I've noticed,' he said.

As her face flushed, he shook his head in a self-deprecating way. 'I've done it again, haven't I? As I said before, I don't mean to be unkind. I've got into a habit of...insensitivity with women.'

'It's all right,' she insisted. Then, like a litany, she mentally went over the many rules for good medicine which she had made for herself, trying to answer his question. While he poured himself coffee, his back to her, Abby took a swallow of hers and collected her thoughts.

'As for my ethics...well, do not force or coerce a patient into having a treatment he or she does not really want, even if the prognosis without it would be poor,' she stated. 'Sometimes "treatments" can kill—many are not without risk. If a patient wants a second, or a third, opinion, before agreeing to a course of treatment or an operation, make sure he or she gets it.'

'Hmm. Go on.' He sipped coffee, eyeing her thoughtfully. Abby had no idea what he was thinking. This was a snatched interlude that must soon be over.

'Know your biases. Even the very best doctors have

them,' she said, hoping that he would not press her further. What, she wondered, were Dr Contini's biases and weaknesses? Maybe finding out would be interesting. 'Try to know your strengths and weaknesses.'

'What do you think of euthanasia?' he asked unexpectedly.

For a few seconds Abby looked at him, sensing something other than curiosity about her opinions in his question, yet she could not have analyzed why she thought that.

'I know that some doctors advocate euthanasia,' she said slowly, averting her gaze from his shrewd perception. This was something that she felt very strongly about. 'I'm not one of them.'

'Tell me why,' he said softly.

'I—I'm not particularly religious,' she said, stammering a little, 'but the admonition "thou shalt not kill" figures very large in my personal philosophy, I guess. I haven't really analyzed it very thoroughly...In my experience, people do not want to have their life taken from them—they want to be relieved of their pain. We all love life, we cling to it.'

'Hmm,' he murmured, watching her.

'To...er...to take a life is extreme arrogance,' Abby went on. 'I deplore arrogance of any kind.'

'I agree with you absolutely. It is not in our mandate to take a life. Not actively.' There was a bleakness in his voice, as though this were a question that he had been forced to consider many times. Abby knew that must have been the case.

Encouraged, she went on and felt her cheeks tinge with warm colour as she disclosed her thoughts, struggling to find the appropriate words. 'To me, the trust that a sick person has in his or her doctor is a sacred trust, never in any circumstances to be breached. As you say, it is not our mandate...We are not in a position to have, or to take, that sort of power over the life of another. It's abhorrent...obscene.'

He nodded, saying nothing. The silence that ensued seemed to be charged with a peculiar understanding between them, as though there had been other questions silently asked and just as silently answered. Yet Abby had no idea, no idea at all, what those questions might be…or what the answers were. She remembered the premonition that she had felt at the medical rounds.

Abby bit her lip indecisively, looking down at the cup that she held in her hand. She wanted to leave, but could not seem to summon up the energy to make the move. Then she felt his fingers touch her own as he grasped the cup.

'Thank you for talking to me,' he said quietly. 'Let me get you more coffee—that must be cold. I've been asking you too many questions, haven't I?' The touch had the effect of deepening the inertia that had come over her. She could not understand herself. Neither did she know why he was thanking her for talking to him.

He handed her back a full cup. 'Here, I won't say another word while you drink that.'

Automatically she added cream and sugar to the hot liquid.

'You ask a lot of questions, rather personal ones, Dr Contini,' she said bravely, not looking at him. 'I wonder if you answer them so freely yourself.'

'Drink your coffee, Dr Gibson,' he said. 'You may not get another chance.' They looked at each other, as they both drank the welcome coffee, sizing each other up. Abby was the first to look away.

'I'd be pleased to answer any questions that you might have,' he offered quietly. 'Another time.'

There were footsteps of someone approaching the door outside, then a knock. 'Ah, there you are, Dr Contini.' A secretary had put her head round the door. 'There's an outside call for you from the Gresham General Hospital. They want to talk to you right away.' She glanced at Abby. 'Shall I put the call through to you here?'

'Yes, please,' he said, after a fraction of hesitation.

When he answered the telephone a moment later, it seemed to Abby that he switched instantly to a totally different mind-set—that he tuned out the present situation, including her, and projected his thoughts totally to whoever was speaking to him. When he looked at her his expression was blank, as though he scarcely saw her, when she made to leave.

'Thank you for coming, Dr Gibson,' he said formally. 'I'll doubtless be talking to you in a few days about Mr Simmons.'

'Thank you, Dr Contini,' she said.

As she walked away from his office, she considered that he might have a cross-appointment at one of the other teaching hospitals in Gresham, the Gresham General, although she was surprised at that. The position at University Hospital was a very demanding one, which, she had assumed, would take up all his time. Maybe he was just being called to a consultation. Gresham General was a hospital that she went to occasionally herself as part of her training program.

Abby felt sober and thoughtful as she left the floor to make her way to Outpatients on the ground level. Going over the case of Mr Simmons in her mind, it was clear that everything possible was going to be done for him to effect a cure. He was in very good hands. There would be unwanted side-effects for him, of course—in order for chemotherapy to be effective, the first dose had to be followed up not long after by a second dose. Such toxic drugs left a person's body susceptible to opportunistic infections.

Abby had to admit that Dr Contini was very good at his job—very good indeed.

Lunch was almost over in the cafeteria when Abby got there late, in the early afternoon, having seen a few more patients.

'Hello, Dr Gibson.' Ginny Ryles, who was coming out, accosted her. 'I'm still here, as you see. Can't seem to drag myself away from the place.'

'I know what you mean.' Abby smiled at her, noting the tiredness on the other woman's face. 'How is he?'

'He's stable,' Mrs Ryles conceded. 'Not in any pain, thank God.'

'Good. If there's anything I can do to help in any way, let me know.' Although she was a junior doctor, with very little political clout, there might be something she could do, with others, about the threatened 'downsizing'—how she hated that word—of the radiology department.

'Well…as far as his job's concerned, you could possibly talk to Blake about that,' Ginny Ryles said tiredly. 'He's been so good to us, even though he's had that awful trouble himself—all that with Kaitlin,' Mrs. Ryles said.

'I…' Abby began, mystified. Who was Kaitlin? she wondered again.

Mrs. Ryles did not give her the opportunity to ask. She was not sure that it was any business of hers anyway. Perhaps the other woman assumed that she knew.

'Who will be advocates for the patients, or for the professional staff, when businessmen are in charge?' Mrs Ryles went on passionately, before moving to take her leave. 'Tell me that!'

CHAPTER FOUR

THOSE words were going round and round inside Abby's head as she made her way back to the clinic later. There was no guarantee that the family practice unit would not be asked to move out of the hospital because of budget cuts—it was not much of a money-maker for the hospital these days. That seemed to be the main criterion for survival. Confusion was a necessary state for a take-over, she realized only too well. And, like most other workers in the hospital at that moment, she was definitely confused. And she had no answers.

Trying to push all that out of her mind for the time being, to concentrate on patient care, she went back to work.

Much later, Abby unlocked the door of her small apartment, juggling three plastic bags of groceries, her attaché case and two dresses covered in thin plastic which she had picked up from the dry-cleaners on the way home from work. She had also managed to carry her compact overnight bag. For the last two nights she had slept in the hospital residence that housed doctors, technicians, nurses, and others who were oncall for nights and weekends. Members of her group took a few, regular, on-calls.

She elbowed the door shut. It was already after seven o'clock. She was tired and her feet were killing her. It had been a very long, tiring day. All she could think of at that moment was getting something to eat and drink—she was starving again.

First dumping everything she was carrying onto the sofa in the sitting room, she went to the tiny kitchen and poured herself a half glass of cool white wine from a bottle that she already had open in the fridge. Wineglass in hand, she sank onto the sofa, slipped off her shoes and put her feet up on the coffee-table.

'Ah…thank God it's Friday,' she said, taking a gulp of wine, then leaning back and closing her eyes with a sigh of pleasure. It would take her more than a few minutes to unwind after the rather hectic day.

Had it really been only this morning when she had found Dr Ryles collapsed in the corridor? It seemed days away, rather than hours. Her meetings with Dr Contini had unsettled her, too; for some reason she could not get his image out of her mind. The fact of that irritated her no end. She wanted to relax over the next two days, not think about work…or about Blake Contini's Celtic good looks, the dark hair contrasting dramatically with the fair skin, the piercing blue eyes, the dark, decisive brows…

'Oh, hell,' she said aloud. 'Stop thinking about him…'

When the telephone rang ten minutes later she knew it would be her friend Cheryl, who lived in the same apartment building.

They had a routine on Friday evenings when they were both off duty. They would take turns to cook supper, then after that they might go out to a street café for an after-dinner coffee, if they were not too exhausted. Sometimes Cheryl would bring a boyfriend, or Abby would bring one of her own. Usually they made up a small group as some of the other young doctors, of both sexes, lived in this apartment building which was convenient for the hospital because it was close to a main subway line. There was no one in particular, no man that she particularly liked. That was the way she wanted to keep it for now.

Languidly she picked up the receiver. 'Yeah, Cheryl, I know it's my turn to get the food,' she said with mock exasperation into the telephone, not bothering to say hello first. 'I've only just got in. You could have waited a bit

longer—I need at least half an hour in which to get in-
ebriated.'

When there was no reply at the other end, she went on,
'It's been a crazy day, with that somewhat overbearing
Blake Contini giving me the runaround. I wish you'd been
there when I had to go up to see the patient. He, Dr Contini,
treated me a bit like a medical student, firing questions at
me—you know, in front of the patient. I suppose I can't
complain…I did learn something.'

She paused for breath and another sip of the wine.
'Mmm…this wine's good. I might just save a bit for you,
Cheryl—especially if you come and help me get the food
ready. How's that for a bribe?' She giggled.

There was silence at the other end.

'Cheryl?' Abby said.

'This is not Cheryl,' a deep, masculine voice said, almost
making Abby jump out of her skin. 'It's the "overbearing
Blake Contini".'

'Oh my God.' Abby sat up quickly, spilling a little of
the wine on her skirt. 'I…had no idea. I'm awfully sorry.
Why—I mean, how did you get my number? And…um…
yes…why?'

Quickly she searched her memory for anything that he
might have asked her to do which she had forgotten. She
wasn't on call again, was she? It was easy to get confused
sometimes when you had been on call for twenty-four
hours, when night seemed to merge into day, with one's
track of time temporarily lost. No…no, she wasn't on call,
she was sure of it. There was nothing else that came immediately to mind.

'Well, Dr Gibson,' he said, 'getting your number wasn't
difficult. I had intended to give you an assignment this
morning, before I got called away.'

Feeling stone cold sober again, having previously
thought that the wine was beginning to help her unwind,
Abby swallowed nervously, taken totally by surprise. Did

she detect a touch—a barely perceptible touch, to be sure—of humour in his voice? She sure hoped so.

Some of the senior men resented having to teach family practice doctors-in-training, as well as those residents in internal medicine who were part of the department proper. She found herself wondering if he was one of those, although she didn't think so. That morning, with Mr Simmons, he had seemed to quietly enjoy the role of mentor, even if he had been a bit overbearing. Maybe he wanted to make quite sure that she had her plateful of work, so to speak.

'Oh…oh, that's all right, then,' she found herself gabbling. 'For a moment I thought I had neglected to do something that you'd asked me.' She gave a laugh. 'I would be pleased, Dr Contini, to have an assignment. Presumably, it would be regarding Mr Simmons? Yes, I'd be absolutely delighted!'

There was another silence, punctuated only by Abby's noisy swallow. She wondered why he was making her feel so nervous. She dealt with senior colleagues—indeed, colleagues at all levels—with a certain professional aplomb, even though she did say it herself. She was almost proud of the way she got along easily with colleagues. Apart from the fact that she had called Dr Contini overbearing, she had an awful feeling that he could be the exception with regard to maintaining her equanimity.

'What exactly was it about my behaviour that you found overbearing, Dr Gibson?' he said.

'Well, I… Really, that was a mistake, sir… I was just sounding off. You know how it is. I thought you were my friend Cheryl,' she managed to say, feeling a certain hysteria rising in her.

'Come on, Dr Gibson,' he said, sarcasm in his voice, 'cough it up. I didn't take you for a shy one. Quite the opposite, in fact.'

This conversation had gone far enough. 'Look, I'm awfully sorry, Dr Contini. I didn't mean it. I have no real criticism of you, or your behaviour. Now, please, I would be very happy to hear about any assignment you may have for me.'

'Nevertheless, I would appreciate an answer to my question,' he said firmly.

As though his penetrating blue eyes could actually see her, Abby found herself flushing. 'All right,' she said. 'It was your assumption, on first seeing me, that I was deliberately late for the rounds, then acting on that assumption. And I am...you know...I am an MD.'

'Hmm. Well, when someone is late I assume that they *are* late, if you see what I mean,' he said. To Abby's heightened perception, it seemed that the very faint touch of humour was back. 'I'm very aware that you're an MD, Dr Gibson. Anyway, I apologize for seeming to be overbearing. It's just that I take my duties very seriously. You would do well to remember that, which, I realize, may sound overbearing to you.'

'That's quite all right,' she said.

He paused. 'Is it?'

'Yes.'

'Good.' He was definitely smiling now, she could tell. 'Now, here's the assignment.'

'Just a moment. Should I write this down?'

He laughed. 'I think you're quite capable of retaining this in your memory, Dr Gibson. I just want you to write me a projection of Mr Simmons's treatment and the possible outcome, starting with the pre-chemo treatment. You saw the blood-work results which, I expect, you will remember as there's nothing very out of the ordinary about them. Typical for his diagnosis...wouldn't you say? It will be standard in your textbook.'

'Yes, I do remember,' Abby said. 'Is that it?'

'That's it.'

'And when do you want it?'

'I'd like it on Monday, if possible, as the treatment is starting right away. I don't want to ruin your weekend, but it shouldn't take you long to do.'

'Yes, all right,' she said, her mind going over all the other things she had planned to do over the weekend—they were mainly chores.

'I'd like you to keep in touch with Mr Simmons's progress,' he said smoothly. 'I think you can learn a lot—and retain it—by following one case through. We're starting the transfusions over the weekend, so when you go to see him on Monday you should see a difference in his condition.'

He was making the assumption that she would have time to see Mr Simmons then. Anyway, she would make the necessary time. She certainly had every intention of keeping in touch with him, although he was Blake Contini's patient, in the general internal medicine department.

'Right,' she said, more businesslike now. 'And I'll make a start on the assignment tomorrow.'

'Could you meet me at eight-thirty on 2 East on Monday morning? I could go over your assignment then.'

'Yes, certainly,' she said, keeping her voice neutral. That took care of her plans to sleep in on Monday, as she did not otherwise have to be at the hospital early. 'I have to be at the clinic at about ten o'clock.'

'That will give us plenty of time.' This time she could definitely hear the smile in his voice. 'Goodnight, Dr Gibson. Have a good weekend.' Was he being sarcastic? She longed to make a stinging retort.

'Um…thank you.' That was all she could think of on the spur of the moment. 'Goodnight.'

He was the first to hang up.

Abby leaned back against the sofa. 'Bloody hell!' she said. 'Why didn't I find out who it was before I opened my big mouth? He must think I'm an absolute klutz now…more so than usual.' She groaned again. For some reason she wanted Blake Contini to think well of her, and it wasn't just because he was so unbearably attractive either.

With a few determined swallows she downed the contents of the wineglass, just as there was a knock on the door. Her eyes were watering and she was coughing when she opened the door to Cheryl.

'What's up? You sick or something?' Cheryl asked. 'If the answer's yes, that's too bad, as far as I'm concerned, because I'm through doctoring for the day.'

'Too much wine. You won't be able to say that,' Abby gasped, between coughs, 'when you're a GP, out in the big, cold world all by yourself.'

'Yeah, well…until that day comes I'm going to keep regular hours whenever I can.' Cheryl grinned, coming into the apartment. 'Where's the food, then? As your phone was busy, I thought I'd just come down to get it.'

'Forever the optimist,' Abby laughed.

'Da-da!' Cheryl whipped a bottle of wine from behind her back. 'This is my contribution.'

'Great! I can sure use that.'

Cheryl had short, curly dark hair, a wide, humorous grin and blue eyes that were invariably good humoured also. She was straightforward and honest, which was why Abby liked her so much. There was never anything bitchy or underhand about her, not like a lot of colleagues of both sexes who treated their peers as though they had to be in constant competition with them.

'The food's not ready yet. I had a call from Dr Contini.'

'What? *The* Dr Contini?' Cheryl was all attention.

'Yep.'

While they prepared a simple supper in the kitchen, Abby told Cheryl all about her day—about the telephone call, about finding Dr Ryles. For once Cheryl kept her mouth shut and just listened, and her eyes were serious.

'You've sure had a weird day,' she commented when Abby stopped talking. 'Will Ryles is a great guy. All sorts of strange things are going on in the hospital, Abby, with all the cost-cutting. I wish I knew what to do about some of them.'

'I know. Likewise.'

'A lot of people don't want to get involved in fighting against it unless they themselves are directly involved in the changes, even though they're as scared as hell,' Cheryl went on emphatically.

'Yeah. It's so convenient to be able to pretend that something isn't real unless it happens to you,' Abby said thoughtfully.

'Convenient, but ultimately crazy,' Cheryl said. 'Talk about fiddling while Rome burns. You know, you have to confront things eventually because we are all eventually affected.'

'"No man is an island entire of itself…"' Abby quoted the familiar lines.

'Right,' Cheryl said.

'Maybe if the family practice unit gets closed down, or shifted somewhere else, our lot will get involved,' Abby said.

'Hmm,' Cheryl mused, 'let's hope so. You know…I think it's a bit odd that Blake would have called you at home. I doubt it's a habit of his. Maybe…just maybe…he likes you, Abby. Even though I expect he's married.'

'Is he?'

'Don't know. I would think so, wouldn't you?'

'Yes.'

'I think someone mentioned, in passing, that he had children. Maybe he's divorced,' Cheryl said musingly.

Abby kept her eyes on the salad she was mixing, chastising herself for the peculiar sense of loss that came over her at the suggestion that Blake Contini might not be free. What did it matter to her, anyway? She had known him for one day, and she could easily find, a couple of weeks from now, that she didn't like him after all. 'Are you on first-name terms with him?' she asked.

'No.' Cheryl laughed. 'Only behind his back. Let's eat. Then we can meet up with some of the other guys and go out for coffee. Something tells me you need a change of scene even more than I do.'

'You're on,' Abby agreed.

'Shall we eat on the balcony?' Cheryl said. 'The temperature went up a lot this afternoon, thank goodness. About time for May.'

'Good idea.'

While Abby took cutlery and plates out to the balcony, where she had a small table and some chairs, Cheryl put the food and wine on a tray. They had a pasta salad, with herbs and olive oil, and a green salad, with crusty bread and cheese.

The tiny apartment was on the third floor of a ten-storey block, overlooking a park, in a pleasant residential area bordering a low-rise street of trendy little shops and restaurants where the street life, the café life, extended well into the night, without being rowdy.

'One day,' she mused to Cheryl, as they looked out over the park, 'I hope to have a house of my own, with a large garden...maybe a dog or two...one day when I have real money of my own, instead of being always on the edge of poverty. I'm so sick of being poor, Cheryl.'

'Who isn't?'

'Of course, poverty is relative. I love this apartment and I have an income of sorts, even if I do owe my soul to the bank and my parents for the cost of my medical training.' She thought of the genuinely homeless people, sleeping in bus shelters or under bridges. Some of those people sometimes made their way to her clinic.

'Better not to dwell on what you owe, just pay up each month. I want all those things that you want, Abby,' Cheryl said, helping herself to pasta, 'and maybe a nice husband to go with it. I'm an old-fashioned girl. Someone like Blake Contini would be nice, eh?' She laughed. 'Chance would be a fine thing! Have some more wine.'

For some reason Abby did not feel like laughing. 'I wish you hadn't said that, Cheryl,' she remarked feelingly. 'I have to be rooted in reality, not in fantasy.' First and foremost she had to earn a living—she had never counted on a husband to help her with that.

'Fancy him, do you?' Cheryl looked at her shrewdly. 'Don't worry, by the time he's been there a couple of months, or less, most of the female population of the hospital will fancy him too. So you'll be in good company.'

'I didn't say I did,' Abby protested.

'Ah, but you would if you'd let yourself, Abby,' Cheryl said succinctly. 'I know you pretty well. Anyway, you're quite a stunner yourself…if you wouldn't act so oblivious to the opposite sex. I've seen guys lusting after you…then you treat them like they're your brothers or something.'

'Oh, bug off!' Abby smiled, hiding the truth behind her friend's words. 'You know, I was with him today in his office when he got a call from Gresham General. I don't know what the call was about…but he just sort of tuned me out completely. Seconds before that he'd been joking…you know.'

'Hmm.' Cheryl murmured, her mouth full of food. 'Maybe one of his kids is sick in there—if he's got kids, that is. Don't let it worry you—you'll find out soon enough.'

They ate in companionable silence, each mulling over events of the day. Abby found that her thoughts persistently came back to the image of Blake Contini and to her verbal *faux pas*. Maybe some good would come out of it, that he knew she found him overbearing. Even then she knew that if she had any dreams, they would be about him…a substitute for reality.

Later that evening, back from having coffee with a group of friends and colleagues at a street café, Abby felt restless. Far from being able to push thoughts of her patients out of her mind, they persistently intruded. Images of Ralph Simmons and the man Gary Barlow, with possible lung cancer, tormented her.

Over the years of training, she had gradually discovered that increasing knowledge and expertise helped to overcome the stress of the job. You could use your knowledge to assess a situation accurately, to know your strengths and weaknesses, to know what you could or could not do with someone who was sick—then you could use your expertise to carry out that which you *could* do.

It was all very positive because, even though you could not always save lives, you knew that you could do your very best. It was that best, maintaining your own standards, that kept the demons at bay, that enabled you to do your job. It also meant referring to someone else, a specialized person, when you knew you could not cope.

Thinking about these things, Abby got out her textbook on general internal medicine, a thick tome, to refresh her memory on the details of acute myelogenous leukemia. In spite of what Dr Contini had said about not wanting to spoil her weekend, he clearly wanted her to have come up with something meaningful by Monday morning. It would not be difficult as she already had a fair knowledge of her subject. Accordingly, she decided to make preliminary notes now.

Rummaging through her attaché case for pens and a pad of paper, she came across a sealed envelope which she did not remember seeing before. Maybe it was something she had had in there for weeks, maybe a copy of a report or something that she had meant to file. There was no name on it so she slit it open. There was a hand-written letter inside, a hasty scrawl.

Dear Blake,

It was good of you to go over the stuff that I left for you to look at. I have since discovered that the Drexler family (a member is on the Board of Directors of the hospital, as you may know) used to own the distance-imaging computer radiology company, Compu-X-ray Services. They made it a public company a while ago. Now I hear that the family is trying to buy back all the shares, with a view to selling the whole company to a similar operation in the States.

Could we meet to talk about this? I have other information about this that I don't want to commit to paper right now. All I can say is that things might not be above board.

The company interested in buying Compu-X-ray Services may be (I have heard a rumour) Image Tec, of the States. It is, I think, Image Tec who want to take over my department—with the approval of Admin., of course. Maybe we have a possible conflict of interest here.

Sincerely, Will

Abby put the letter down slowly on her dining table, realizing that she had automatically read the letter through…a private letter that had nothing to do with her.

It had been intended for Blake Contini, obviously, and must have fallen out of one of Will Ryles's pockets with the other stuff that she had picked up. The cellular telephone and other items she had given to the nurses in the coronary care unit.

'Damn!' Abby said out loud.

Here was another source of embarrassment for her where Blake Contini was concerned. Of course, she could put the letter in another envelope and pretend that she had not read it, but she felt sure that she would betray herself. She was no good at subterfuge of any sort. No, better just to tell him that she had inadvertently read it. Tomorrow she would have to call him.

Maybe Will Ryles would be wondering about that letter—whether it had got into the wrong hands. It appeared that he had been doing some investigating of private companies who were hoping to take over some of the hospital's radiology functions.

Forcing all that out of her mind, she opened her medical textbook to the section 'Hematology and Oncology', putting her pen and paper at the ready.

She waited until half past ten the next morning before she plucked up courage to call Blake Contini's home number, having got it from the locating service at the hospital. It was possible that Saturday was one day of the week when he slept late, she told herself nervously as she waited for someone to answer his ringing telephone. Maybe the letter from Dr Ryles was not important and could wait until Monday, but she felt guilty for having read it and anxious to hand it over to him.

'Hello.' He answered the call himself. Abby felt absurdly relieved.

'Hello, Dr Contini,' she said quickly. 'This is Dr Gibson. Um...I'm sorry to call you on a weekend. It's just that I found a letter in my bag for you from Dr Ryles. I must have picked it up in the basement corridor. I'm afraid I inadvertently read it...there was no name on the envelope, you see. I'm awfully sorry about that.' In the short time she had known him, she had been apologizing rather a lot.

'Good morning, Dr Gibson,' he said. He sounded relaxed, as though he had just got out of bed. 'What was the gist of it?'

'Something about Image Tec and Compu-X-ray Services,' she said.

'Hmm...' There was a short silence. 'Could I come to

pick it up from wherever you are? I would rather like to have it soon.'

'Yes.' Abby gave him her address and brief instructions on how to get to her place from where he lived.

She noted that he lived in an old established, wealthy neighbourhood, not actually very far in driving time from where she was living, which was itself an old neighbourhood of mainly artisans' cottages from the last century, as well as some older mansions that had fallen upon hard times.

'I live in one of the few apartment buildings in this immediate area,' she said.

'I'll be there within the half-hour, if that's convenient for you,' he said.

'Yes, it is.'

'Maybe you could give me a cup of coffee, Dr Gibson, since I haven't had my morning coffee yet. Hmm?'

'I think I could manage that,' she said. 'I'm pretty handy in the kitchen.'

'I'm sure you are.' He was laughing at her again; Abby could sense rather than hear a lightening in his tone. Maybe he wasn't such an ogre after all. Yet somehow his amusement annoyed her.

Fortunately she had cleaned and tidied the small apartment earlier in the week before she had been on call for the two nights. Frequently it was something of a mess— there was never enough time for housekeeping. Nevertheless, she looked around hastily, picked up a newspaper, plumped up a few cushions.

The sitting room was an eclectic mixture of furniture from garage sales, the purview of the underfunded, Abby acknowledged with a rueful smile as she looked at each well-loved item.

There were also junk-shop finds, plus odds and ends that her family and friends had donated to her when she had got her own place at the start of her internship. The walls

of the sitting room she had painted a rich dark green, which
made the place feel warm and intimate in winter, cool and
shady in summer. What she lacked in furniture she made
up for with potted plants, family photographs in interesting
frames and lots of books.

Abby finished tidying up quickly, then hurried to the
bathroom to put on a bit of make-up and subdue her unruly
hair, feeling a little nervous that her senior colleague would
see her in her own somewhat humble setting. She was used
to 'humble' herself; often she even preferred it that way. It
often came as a surprise to her to discover that some people
were particularly snobbish about material possessions—or,
rather, a lack of them in other people's lives. It was awful,
she thought, to be judged by what you owned.

As she scrutinized her face in the mirror and ran a brush
through her thick hair that was curling in tendrils around
her face and neck, she thought of her girlhood spent at a
private co-ed day school for which she had won scholar-
ships, where she had been known, usually affectionately,
as 'The Brain' among her peers.

As she secured her hair behind her head with an elastic
band, then carefully applied a little lipstick and eye shadow,
she thought of those days of single-minded effort, when
she had not dared to let her standards slip for fear that she
would not be awarded a scholarship the following year.

She smiled at her reflection thoughtfully. For the most
part, her school years had been very happy. When friends
of hers had introduced her to others, they had almost invariably said, 'This is Abby...she's a "brainer", a natural.'
She had always smiled modestly and shrugged. Maybe she
was a 'natural', yet success never came easily, you still had
to work very hard. No one had ever handed her anything
on a plate.

The doorbell rang just as Abby had the coffee made. As
she hurried to the intercom in the hallway of her flat, she
chided herself for being as nervous as the schoolgirl she

had once been. Although she had had boyfriends at school, at medical school and beyond, and brief affairs, she knew that she had always held back, had never been totally in love. Sometimes she was aware that her reluctance to get involved might make her seem standoffish to men…

'Hi. Blake Contini,' the voice said abruptly as she answered the intercom.

'I'll let you in,' she said, and buzzed open the outer door.

In the few minutes that he took to come up three floors in the elevator, she carried the coffee and cups into the sitting room.

'Good morning,' Abby said, as she opened her door to let him in. There was an odd feeling of dissonance in her as she saw him standing there in the corridor outside her apartment. Yesterday at the medical rounds, when he had so annoyed her, she would not have imagined that he would today be entering her home.

'Good morning again,' he said, smiling slightly.

From her face down to her feet, which were clad in simple sandals, his eyes went over her quickly, so that she found herself feeling hot with unaccustomed self-consciousness. Professional training made one self-aware, hopefully, but usually decreased self-consciousness. Nonetheless, she wished he would not assess her quite so openly, or with such devastating astuteness.

He wore casual cotton pants, pressed and neat, in a light stone colour, with a loose dark green sweater over a check shirt, an outfit that matched her own jeans and simple blouse. The immediate impression she had of him was of relaxed sophistication.

'Come in, Dr Contini,' she said, standing aside so that he could pass. 'I have coffee ready.'

'I'm looking forward to it,' he said.

In the sitting room she handed over the letter. 'I apologize again for having read it. I didn't immediately realize who ''Blake'' was…so I couldn't figure out who it was for right away.'

'Maybe you'd better call me Blake, then,' he said, with an ironic smile, taking the letter out of the torn envelope, 'Simpler and less formal.' In a few seconds he had scanned the scrawled lines.

'Poor old Will.' He'd murmured the words.

'Would you like some coffee?' she asked politely.

'Please,' he said a little absently. 'I'm desperate for coffee.'

While she poured two cups of coffee, she noted that he glanced quickly around her cosy, lived-in sitting room. 'How is Dr Ryles?' she asked. 'Have you had any up-to-date news of him?'

'Yes. I called the unit this morning. They said he had a good night, that he's alert and talking with the staff. If he gets over this episode, hopefully he'll be fine.'

'I do hope so.'

'I'm glad you called me about the letter,' he said, helping himself to cream and sugar. 'I'd also be grateful if you didn't mention the contents to anyone. Dr Ryles has been discussing his professional problems with me over the past few months—in confidence. I, and a few other people, have been trying to help him.'

'Of course I won't mention it to anyone. It's really nothing to do with me,' Abby said, very aware of how his masculine presence seemed to fill her sitting room like a dynamic force.

Through the open door of the balcony a fresh, warm breeze came into the room. 'May I go outside? It's a great day,' he said.

'Yes, please, do.'

They both stood outside, looking out over the park where the grass was green from spring rain and more recent sunshine. 'It's a terrible shame what's happening at the hospital now,' Abby said tentatively. 'So much secrecy…and no real control by the people who actually do the jobs.'

He looked at her thoughtfully, unsmiling. 'Yes,' he said. In the harsh light of day she saw again the subtle signs of strain on his face and wondered why, apart from the fact that he worked very hard—as did almost everyone else she knew.

Standing a few feet away from her colleague, Abby sipped hot coffee thoughtfully. She felt intuitively that he, too, held much of himself back, as she did, with the opposite sex. Yet he was warm and giving with his patients. There was something about him, a maturity, that drew her to him emotionally. Usually she knew young men her own age who were less mature than she was herself. She felt a desire to know more about him…much more.

'May I help myself to more coffee?' his request broke into her thoughts.

'Yes, sure, Dr Contini,' she smiled.

'Call me Blake,' he said. 'It's easier.'

'All right.'

'And I'll call you Abby, shall I? Or Abigail?'

'Whichever you like,' she said with a little shrug, trying not to let him see how much she liked his company. Maybe, after all, he was married.

'Abigail. That's a very pretty name,' he murmured, looking at her closely, as though he wanted to memorize her features.

Not as pretty as Kaitlin. The thought popped into Abby's head spontaneously, surprising her, especially as she had no idea who Kaitlin was.

They moved back to the sitting room for more coffee. Near her desk, piled with books and papers, she had a small wooden shelf, attached to the wall, on which she kept memorabilia from her schooldays. Blake's glance moved over it, coming to rest on a polished wooden shield with small silver plaques attached to it.

Going closer, he read aloud from it: '"Awarded to the student who has the highest academic standing in the senior school for the year…"' His voice trailed off as he continued to read, then he turned to look at her. 'Abigail Gibson…four years in a row. Well, I certainly have no reason to be overbearing with you, do I?'

Abby flushed. 'I wish you could forget I said that,' she muttered.

'I shall probably get a little more mileage out of that, just for fun…Abby. With all that…' he nodded towards the wooden shield '…I think I might well need it.'

When he smiled, Abby found herself staring at him, their eyes locked together in a mutual regard that held a new tension in it. This was the first time he had given her all his undivided attention in a personal way out of a hospital setting. The effect was devastating.

'I…hope you didn't think I had just squeaked through medical school and wanted to become a GP because I couldn't get into a speciality,' she said, forcing herself to dampen the attraction she felt. 'Some doctors do think that about those of us who choose family practice.' The reality for her had been that many of her teachers at university had tried to recruit her into their own specialities, but she had adamantly stuck to her original intention of becoming a family doctor.

'No,' he said softly, 'nothing like that.'

'Having a good brain can be a great compensating factor, as I expect you know,' she said.

'And what do you have to compensate for, Abby?' he asked softly. 'You are also beautiful.' His glance settled on her mouth so that she felt an absurd desire to sway forward so that he could kiss her.

'You'd be surprised. We all have our burdens,' she said.

'Mmm.'

Abby reached for a plate of biscuits that she had put on the table. 'Have a cookie,' she offered.

'No, thanks. I really have to go now.' He put his cup down. It was almost as though he had switched off suddenly, as though his friendliness had been an aberration. 'That coffee was delicious. Thank you.'

Desperately sorry that the interlude was over, Abby hid her slight agitation by gathering up the cups and other coffee things on the table.

'Let me help before you drop that,' he said lightly, alluding to her clumsiness of the day before—teasing her. She allowed him to take some of the things out of her hands.

In the tiny, windowless kitchen they placed the used items beside the sink. 'Well, I'll see you on Monday, Abby,' he said. 'Thank you again.'

'My pleasure,' she said, turning towards him.

As she turned, he surprised her by bending forward to kiss her, she supposed, on the cheek. Startled, she jerked sideways awkwardly in agitation so that as he came close her lips brushed his mouth. The sound of her sharp, betraying intake of breath filled the silent room. Instantly he had tensed. She sensed it rather than saw it as her eyes searched his face. They were very close now, their faces still only inches apart.

The air of intense strain was on him again as he looked down at her, his eyes blazing into hers. Involuntarily Abby's lips, tingling with the touch of him, parted for his kiss. More than anything she wanted to ease that strain, to ask him what it meant. The smoldering sexual tension, which had started between them almost from the moment they had met, threatened now to burst into a conflagration of passion, sweeping them with it. With its sudden, unfamiliar power, it caught her off guard.

'I…' Abby took a step back, feeling the hard rim of the counter top against her back.

'Abby…' There was such longing in his voice as he said her name that she knew what she would do. Intuitively, she knew that he had not held a woman in his arms for a long time, that he needed her.

'Oh, God…' The sound was torn from her as she reached to put her arms around his neck. She felt her body sway towards his as though she were watching someone else, felt herself lift up her face to his.

For a moment he stiffened again, then, with a groan of abject need, he pulled her into his arms, gripping her, straining her against his body, crushing her mouth with his in a kiss of desperate hunger.

His mouth moved on hers, parting her soft lips, as though he wanted to take her sweetness into himself, overpowering her. Willingly she clung to him, her hands moving up into his thick hair, her fingers combing through it as she held his head down to her.

Around her body his arms were like bands of steel, holding her as though he never wanted to release her. For a long time they kissed, their mouths clinging for long moments of ecstasy, breaking away to move over cheeks, then back to warm mouths. Abby found herself trembling, her lips seeking his again and again, letting him support her weight.

'Abby…' he murmured her name between demanding kisses. 'Abby…' Then his hands found the bare skin of her back, sliding up warmly under her loose blouse. His touch gentled as he caressed her, and she pressed forward in acquiescence, her eyes closed.

Abby lost track of time. It could have been seconds or hours; she was aware only of the feel of him, that she wanted this to go on for ever.

CHAPTER FIVE

IT HAD been the telephone, inevitably, that had pulled them apart and brought them back to a more sober reality.

Thinking about it later, when Abby was again alone, the interlude of abandon seemed like a dream. Yet the physical and emotional agitation that remained with her as she alternately sat and then paced the room reminded her that it had been only too real.

'You're not on call, are you?' Blake had murmured as they had tensed with the ringing of the infernal gadget.

'N-no.' She had whispered the word against his cheek as he held her.

'Ignore it, then,' he had said.

At long last he had pulled away from her, his face vulnerable with desire as he had looked down at her. Unashamedly she had looked back, knowing that she mirrored his need. Uncharacteristically, she had let herself go.

'I definitely must leave this time, sweet Abigail,' he murmured, 'otherwise we'll end up in bed...for the whole day. As much as I would like that, I think it's a little premature, don't you?'

There was an ironic twist to his mouth, letting her know that this was not a habit of his—to get involved with nubile young women with whom he worked. At least, not on such short acquaintance. She buried her hot face in the wool of his sweater, hoping he would know without having to be told that it was not a habit of hers either to get involved with senior colleagues so readily. There was, she felt, just such an understanding between them. Silently, feeling bereft, she nodded her agreement, not trusting her voice.

After a few moments he left. She watched him walk

along the corridor to the elevator that would take him to the ground floor. He moved easily, relaxed and confident. In spite of his sophistication, there was an elemental sexuality about him, an understated sensuality that, she knew, could devastate a woman. He was like a panther—dark, sinuous, awesome and rare. With that image in her mind, Abby closed the door to block him out.

Now she paced, alternately twisting her hands together and letting her arms drop loosely at her sides, not knowing what to do with herself as her churning mind was totally occupied with the image and the remembered feel of him in her arms.

Agitatedly, she went to the kitchen and began to wash the used cups. When that was done, she went around the already tidy apartment, straightening things that did not have to be straightened, folding towels, putting away clothes. She jumped when the telephone rang.

'Hello?' she said tentatively.

'Abby.' Blake's voice sent a wave of heat through her, made her heart beat at a crazy rate. Glad that he was not there to see the flood of colour that suffused her, she wondered at the speed with which her cool sophistication could abandon her. 'I forgot to tell you something.'

'Um…not another assignment!' she managed to groan, something of her usual quick-witted response, albeit a little sluggish, coming to her rescue.

He laughed, his voice husky, as though he was, perhaps, dwelling on the feel of her in his arms. 'I'm having a garden party,' he said, 'a sort of glorified barbecue, at my house in two weeks' time. It's for all doctors in my department and those affiliated. It's a chance for me to get to know the members of my department socially, and for them to know me. I'd like you to be there, Abby, if you would like to come. It won't be formal.'

'Well…yes, I'd like to,' Abby said.

For a few seconds she felt that she was back at school,

receiving an invitation from a class-mate who lived in a mansion, comparing it with the modest house in which her parents lived. She had accepted the invitations then—it would have been churlish not to do so—but knowing that she could not compete socially with them. She had competed with her intellect. It had come naturally to her. She had inspired awe as prizes showered upon her. In a school of high achievers, none of it had been assured.

If only now she could let up a little, relax, and know that not only could she earn her own living, she could help her family as well. Soon…very soon, she could let go her iron will. Even now, with Blake Contini, there were cracks in it. Only one more year to go.

'I'll let you know the details next week,' he said. 'My secretary will be printing up the invitations. And, please, Abby, keep in mind what I said about the confidentiality of the letter. That's very important. Some people who care about the running-down of the hospital hope to start some sort of resistance.'

'Of course.' An idea came to her that perhaps he had invited her to his garden party, to a temporary inner circle, as a subtle pressure on her to keep quiet about the letter. If so, he was underestimating her level of integrity.

'Goodbye, Abby.'

'Goodbye.'

Time to get down to work. At the dining table, a rickety junk shop buy, she began to make notes on her pad, forcing her mind away from Blake. She scanned the printed lines on the open page of her textbook. She wrote down the names of the three powerful broad-spectrum antibiotics that she would give her leukemia patient in sequence. First, she would give intravenous ampicillin…or perhaps Ancef… every six hours. This would be followed by Flagyl three times a day, then Gentomycin every eight to twelve hours. If these drugs failed to rid the body of infection, there was Vancomycin, which could be given prophylactically for twenty-four hours.

Abby bit the end of her pen thoughtfully and gazed into space, seeing in her mind's eye Mr Simmons in his bed, the IV fluids running into his veins, the antibiotics mixed in with them.

In addition to those drugs, she would give the blood transfusions, the packed cells, the platelets that these patients so badly needed to help their blood to clot as it should...yes, she would give that, and also some IV infusions of fresh-frozen plasma, which was necessary to return the blood chemistry to as near normal as possible. The effects of all these things would be short-lived unless the disease was nipped in the bud, thus the need for the chemotherapy.

Abby bent over the paper and wrote busily. They would start the chemo when Mr Simmons had been built up as much as possible. Then within two days all his hair would have fallen out, he would feel nauseated, would vomit— would probably feel more awful than he had ever felt in his life. Then he would question whether it was all worth it. Then she, Abby, and all his doctors and nurses would have to do all that they could to keep his spirits up...as well as their own.

On Monday she was scheduled to visit some inpatients in the morning, then a little later she would join a clinic with one of the family practice unit doctors, Eliza Cruikshank. Just after lunch she had a lecture at the university, a short walk away from the hospital. Cheryl Clinton would be going with her.

Dr Cruikshank always had an interesting mix of patients from all walks of life, both adults and children. Abby looked forward to her clinics. Eliza Cruikshank was her mentor.

On Monday Abby managed to put in place a veneer of sophistication as she entered the hospital early in the morning, encountered the familiar sights, sounds and smells, although she found herself fearing that it would crumble at the sight of Blake in the hospital corridors.

Then there he was, at the nursing station on 2 East, when she got there. Although she had taken great care to be there on time, Blake was already looking through the data on the main computer in the nursing office, probably getting print-outs of the latest lab results on Mr Simmons and other patients he had on the unit. It was the presence of nurses, busily walking in and out of the office, that enabled her to keep control of the initial flush that she felt tinging her cheeks.

Taking a deep breath, Abby went in quietly to stand beside him and look at the screen, feeling a not entirely welcome frisson of physical awareness.

'Good morning, Abby,' he said, turning to look at her. His eyes went over her thick, soft hair, already escaping in tendrils from the elastic band that pulled it back from her face, then quickly over her face, as though he wanted to renew acquaintance with each feature. It was as though he were stripping away her pretences, ones she didn't know she had.

'Glad you could make it,' he went on, turning his attention back to the computer screen. 'I'm just getting the latest results. We've got the results of the liver-function tests and the renal-function tests on Mr Simmons. Two of the medical residents are going to join us to see the patient—they should be here in a few minutes. I'll go over your assignment before they get here.'

Abby thought that he looked tired, pale and somehow more remote than he had been when he had visited her apartment. Maybe he had been on call yesterday.

'I've got it here,' she said, fishing the few sheets of typed paper out of her attaché case, fumbling a little.

As she stood next to him while he looked over her material, she realized that, uncharacteristically, she wanted his approval. She wanted it very much. Usually she did her best, then did not worry too much about how she was judged. Now, looking at Dr Contini's bent head, his serious profile, she wanted to see him smile again, the way he had after he had looked at the evidence of her school achievements.

'Good,' he said, scrutinizing her notes. 'Mr Simmons has already started the courses of the antibiotics you have suggested here. We keep the Vancomycin as the pièce de résistance, of course, in case he doesn't respond to the others.' He turned over a page. 'Now…what have you proposed for the chemo…?' He continued to read. 'I see you make the comment here that partial remission offers no substantial survival benefit. Yes…and that remission rates in adults are inversely related to age. Mmm…'

'During the induction chemo,' Abby interjected, 'I've assumed that you would continue the aggressive transfusion support with the fresh-frozen plasma and the platelets. The induction therapy will be for five to ten days, with the chemotherapy drugs.'

'Mmm…' he said.

'Have you…have you heard how Dr Ryles is this morning, Dr Contini?'

'I thought we agreed that you would call me Blake, Abby?'

'Well, yes. It's a little awkward…when I don't know you very well,' she said.

'I expect we'll get to know each other quite well over the next few weeks and months,' he said, looking at her steadily. There was a warmth in his regard, and a few seconds of sexual awareness, before he looked away. 'I called in at the coronary unit earlier. Will Ryles is stabilized. Maybe this will be the enforced rest that he desperately needs.'

'Yes,' she said. His was not a studied charm, she decided… She attempted to distance herself from him mentally, concentrating on the computer printouts she held in her hand.

They were joined then by the two medical residents, Tim Barrick and Alison Lupino, whom Abby knew reasonably well. 'Hi.' She smiled at them, relieved that the initial moment of tension with Blake was over.

'Dr Gibson.' Blake Contini addressed her. 'Why don't you go in to see Mr Simmons? I know you have other things to do. We'll join you in about five minutes. I'll keep your papers…and see you about them at the next medical rounds. I want to take plenty of time with Mr Simmons— to build him up before we start the chemo, to get the balance exactly right, to continue that at the same time as the chemo.'

'Yes.' She nodded agreement. 'Thank you.'

Once she was suitably gowned and gloved to protect the patient against any bacteria that she might introduce into his environment, she entered his room.

'Morning.' Mr Simmons was the first to speak, turning his head towards her as she entered, 'Dr Gibson, isn't it? It's nice to see someone. I'm feeling a bit as though I'm in a space shuttle, in here on my own.'

'Good morning. Yes, I'm Dr Gibson. How are you? You certainly look much better than you did when I saw you a few days ago. I'm amazed.'

The man grinned. 'I feel better, too,' he confirmed, 'even though I know it's going to be short-lived. I haven't felt this good for quite a while.'

Abby scrutinized the three bags of fluid that hung from IV poles attached to the bed frame, the contents dripping slowly into the patient's veins via fine tubes. One contained blood platelets, one plasma, while the third was a clear fluid which Abby could see, was normal saline. The saline line had small piggyback bags of the intravenous antibiotics attached to it, dripping the precious drugs into his bloodstream—drugs that would kill the bacteria that had caused his low-grade lung infection and the intestinal tract infection. His body had gradually lost its natural ability to fight these invading organisms unaided.

'Your colour's good.' Abby smiled at him, most of her face hidden behind her mask. He had lost a lot of that sickly yellow tinge to his skin which had marked him as a seriously ill man, his eyes were more alert, his manner more lively.

'What are my chances, Dr Gibson, of coming out of this alive?' Mr Simmons looked at her directly, his intelligent eyes meeting hers. Still a very handsome man, he had a commanding presence in spite of his condition. He would not want to be cajoled or lied to, yet one always had to choose one's words very carefully because those words from a doctor always came with real or implied authority.

'Well, Mr Simmons,' she said, not flinching, knowing that he would have already asked others these same questions, 'I would be lying to you if I were to minimize the seriousness of this illness. What you have is life-threatening…I'm sure you know that. After the induction chemotherapy you are going to feel very, very sick.'

'Yes… I'm trying to psych myself up for that…it isn't easy.'

'You may relapse after that so it's likely that you'll need a second round of chemotherapy fairly soon after the first—that's called consolidation or intensification chemotherapy,' Abby said, keeping her voice matter-of-fact. 'The first consolidation chemo is usually given four to six weeks after the induction chemo. You'll be in hospital then about four weeks.'

'Mmm. I'll be in about six weeks this time? Right?'

'Yes. You'll probably need a second consolidation chemo,' Abby went on, 'after another four-week interval.'

'In here for another four weeks…right?'

'Yes.'

'Sounds as though I'm going to have to make a career of this,' he said ruefully.

Wanting to comfort him in some way, Abby considered that the best way was to answer his questions as openly as she could, while conveying some optimism, some hope. 'There are some excellent drugs available now, Mr Simmons,' she said. 'There's every reason to be positive.'

Nonetheless, unspoken questions hung in the air, ones he was afraid to ask her. Instinctively she knew that he would have already asked similar questions of other doctors, over and over again. By asking her, he was hoping to get another slant on the answers, thus enabling himself to build up a rounded picture that would bring him closer to the truth and a better idea of his chances. After the consolidation therapy he would be, she knew, in a very delicate situation.

'Dr Contini intends to keep up the transfusions and the antibiotics throughout your other treatment, which will strengthen the chances of a good outcome,' Abby said decisively. 'The transfusions will compensate for the fact that you will have essentially very little effective bone marrow in your body after the chemo.'

'Yes…I see,' he said thoughtfully.

'Rest assured,' she said, 'that a very individual treatment regime will be worked out for you by Dr Contini and the hematologists. No two patients are exactly alike. Nothing will be left to chance. You'll get the very best, the very latest treatment that we have.'

Mr Simmons seemed to relax somewhat. From his semi-sitting position, his body seemed to subside further into the bed, and he gave a muted sigh. 'Well, I've worked with worse odds…' he murmured.

Although both his hands were encumbered with intra-venous lines, Mr Simmons managed to open a drawer in his bedside table and extract a framed photograph.

Silently he handed the photograph to Abby. It showed a young woman with shoulder-length dark hair, attractive, smiling. With her were two young children, a girl of about four and a boy slightly older. 'My family,' Ralph Simmons said quietly.

As Abby was about to ask if that was his daughter and his grandchildren, he spoke again. 'That's my wife and children.'

Hiding her surprise well, Abby kept her eyes lowered to the photograph, feeling an aching sadness as the bright, innocent eyes of the children smiled back at her.

'I have an older family, too,' he said, somewhat unnecessarily.

It was a familiar story—the divorced professional man, in a good financial position to acquire a new, much younger wife, young enough to be his daughter, who then became ill a few years later.

She had seen it so many times before. There would be a few, all too brief years of renewed youth for the man, the illusion of a long, shared life ahead, then the husband's true biological age would assert itself, together with his genetic inheritance where disease was concerned. His children, who should have been his grandchildren, would watch helplessly while their father became the elderly man that his cells proclaimed him to be.

'They're beautiful,' Abby said truthfully, referring to the children.

There were sounds of the other doctors putting on protective gear in the anteroom, so Abby handed back the photograph.

'As I'm a family practice resident I won't be seeing you every day, Mr Simmons,' she said, 'but I will be in as often as possible. Ask Dr Contini anything you want. He can be a little...what shall I say? intimidating at times...perhaps because he's so good at his job. But don't hesitate to voice any concerns.' She was prattling a little, she knew, to hide her reaction to the sight of his family. It was probable that her patient knew Dr Contini better than she did herself.

Ralph Simmons put the photograph away. It was his turn to smile. 'Sounds as though you admire the guy,' he commented astutely, glancing at her. Without intending to, he had effectively taken her off her high horse, so to speak. As she had judged him to be inappropriately married to a very young woman, he had in turn picked up vibes from her with regard to Blake Contini.

'Perhaps I do,' she admitted, not wanting to add that he annoyed her in some way also, 'although I don't know him well. We just met last week. Let's just say that I'm prepared to be impressed. You're in very good hands, Mr Simmons.'

'Yes, I know. What drugs will I be getting for the nausea, by the way...when it starts? I'm not looking forward to that. Always did hate being sea-sick...awful feeling!'

'Well, you usually get stemetil, decadron and maxeran, given intravenously. They're pretty good.'

'I sure hope so. Come to see me as soon as you get the chance, Dr Gibson. I shall rely on it... Otherwise I'll go mad in this space shuttle.'

'I will,' she promised, just as the others came through the door. 'Goodbye for now.'

'Thanks a million.'

'I'm afraid I have to leave, Dr Contini,' she said. 'I have to see three patients on the floors, then go to a clinic.'

'Right.' He nodded at her briskly. 'We'll meet here, no doubt. And at the next medical rounds.' If she had half expected him to say something more personal to her that the others could not hear, she was doomed to disappointment.

'Yes.' Quietly she slipped out. She did not want to hear Mr Simmons asking the same questions, although it was possible that Blake had already given his considered opinion.

As she took off the enveloping gown, she thoughtfully acknowledged how difficult it was, having been passionately kissed by someone, to carry on afterwards as though it had not happened. Perversely, she found herself longing for a future closeness.

Glancing at her watch, she saw that she still had plenty of time in which to see the three inpatients. There might be time for a quick swallow of coffee from the cafeteria before she went to Dr Cruikshank's clinic. Walking briskly away, she found herself looking ahead to the next internal medical rounds—they were held every second Friday. If she did not run into Blake Contini before then, she would definitely see him there.

As she ran down flights of stairs, rather than waiting for the slow elevators, Abby chided herself for speculating on when she would see him again.

'Cut it out!' she said out loud in the empty stairwell. Maybe she was losing her grip, her dedication. Now that the finishing post was in sight, the end of her post-grad training, she was beginning to loosen up prematurely.

Dr Eliza Cruikshank was waiting for her when she finally got to the clinic in the family practice unit in Outpatients, having had her coffee.

'Get your ass in here, Gibson,' Dr Cruikshank said good-humouredly in her raucous voice as Abby entered her office. 'The waiting room's busting at the seams and I'm expecting half a dozen old dears from my diabetic clinic who didn't show last week. I told them to come today or else I was finished with them for good, that I didn't just want to see them when they had messed up their diets, or hadn't bothered to buy their blood test kits for three weeks.'

Abby grinned, taking her lab coat out of her bag and putting it on. Dr Cruikshank had dark, coarse hair which was wavy and generally stood on end untidily. It went well with her rather sallow complexion and dark eyes, and perfectly suited her eccentric, forceful character. She tended to wear shapeless clothes in silk and velvet, often of exotic colours such as crimson and deep purple. There was nothing tentative about Eliza Cruikshank yet she was surprisingly intuitive, compassionate and gentle under her forth-right manner.

'Where do you want me?' Abby said.

'Take the room next door,' Dr Cruikshank said. 'I've left a pile of charts for you there on the desk. And I haven't given you all the old crocks either. There are several new patients in there, including a sixteen-year-old girl who's pregnant. I thought she might want to see someone nearer her own age initially. When you've seen her, you can call me in for a consultation and we'll decide between us what to do with her…taking her views into consideration, of course.'

'Thanks very much!' Abby said, with exaggerated sarcasm, knowing how far she could go with Eliza Cruikshank. 'Is the girl homeless?'

'No, she isn't. Comes from a well-off family. Goes to a private school and all that. Daddy would never forgive her if he knew, apparently. I feel really sorry for the kid. Probably the usual story—plenty of money and material things, not enough love and attention in the home. One extreme to the other, eh? It's a bit of a tricky one, Abby. But aren't they all?'

'Yes,' Abby agreed soberly, gearing herself up mentally for what she would have to encounter in this general clinic, which would produce for them a broad slice of humanity—warts and all, as the expression went.

'By the way, I'm hearing good things about the new chief of medicine,' Dr Cruikshank said as Abby opened the door to go to her own office. 'What's his name…?'

'Dr Contini.'

'That's it. Now…where have I heard that name before?' Eliza Cruikshank frowned. 'Seems I heard it just recently somewhere…maybe at Gresham General… A patient perhaps? Anyway, if we need to refer patients to anyone, we might try a few with him. I had been referring a lot to Gresham General as our old chief was away so much.'

'Ok,' Abby agreed as she went out, not lingering long enough to be an object of Dr Cruikshank's acute perceptiveness, giving no indication that she had met the new chief. And she would have to get a move on if she were to get to the lecture on time later.

Having gone quickly through the pile of case-history charts that had been left in her small office, Abby decided to see the pregnant girl first, who at that moment must be waiting nervously in the crowded waiting room, fearful of what would happen to her. Usually they dealt with pregnant women in the family practice unit, referring them to an obstetrician later when necessary, or to a gynecologist if they chose to terminate the pregnancy.

Taking a deep, steadying breath, then letting it out slowly, Abby went out to the waiting room to call the girl's name. There was not a great deal of privacy in the waiting room. No doubt the girl would be apprehensive that she would be recognized. Probably she had a family doctor, but had chosen not to go to him or her.

'Kyra Trenton,' she said into the waiting room. The girl who got up was tall, very attractive, looking more sophisticated than her sixteen years. She wore blue jeans of an expensive brand, with a loose top. Blonde hair was pulled back and secured in a knot at the back of her head.

'I'm Dr Abby Gibson. I'm with the family practice training program,' Abby said, extending her hand to the girl when they were back in her office. 'Dr Cruikshank has asked me to see you initially, then she'll see you herself.'

The girl shrugged and nodded. 'All right,' she said.

'Have a seat there by the desk,' Abby smiled, then sat down herself, the slim file in front of her on the desk. Like many sixteen-year-olds, this one had a certain worldly veneer which only very slightly disguised the fact that she was little more than a child, even though her height and the touch of make-up that she wore made her seem older.

She had a flawless skin, and looked well nourished and well groomed.

'Are you still at school, Kyra?' Abby began, guessing that this girl would be destined for university.

'Yes,' Kyra said, meeting Abby's gaze frankly, then looking down at the floor and biting her lip. Emotions were very close to the surface at times like this, Abby knew, in spite of the girl's apparent calm. She would have to go carefully, gently.

'Two more years left to do?'

The girl nodded.

'Now…' Abby looked down at the chart. 'I understand that you're pregnant. Can you tell me the first day of your last menstrual period…if you remember it? And I want to know whether that was a normal period in terms of duration and heaviness of flow.'

'Yes…' Kyra's voice was a little above a whisper as she gave the date and described her period as normal. She had probably prepared herself to meet censure, had been prepared to display a certain defiance. Abby was neutral, empathetic, as she wrote down the information.

Abby then looked at the desk calendar. 'You've only missed one period, then, Kyra?'

'Yes.'

'I see. And have you done a pregnancy test?'

'I did the urine test…the one that you can buy from the drug store.' Kyra shifted uneasily in her seat, fidgeting a little with the casual bag that she held on her lap.

'I will have to confirm that myself, by repeating the test,' Abby explained, 'so I'll want a specimen of your urine. Now, Kyra…assuming that you are pregnant, are you intending to have the baby?'

'No…no, I can't,' the girl said softly, looking at the floor again. 'I haven't told my parents. I haven't told anyone before coming here. Not even my best friend. You see, my…my father's a member of parliament in the federal government. I can't let anyone know about this. The newspapers would make a big deal out of this if they knew. Besides, my parents would be horrified.'

'Have you told your mother?'

'No. She's in Ottawa with my father. I'm a weekly boarder at school, and I go home at weekends…most weekends.'

'I see. Is Dr Cruikshank your family doctor?'

'No. He's an old man…the one my parents send me to for my immunizations. I don't want him to know…please.' Kyra suddenly looked frightened, as her vulnerable blue eyes made visual contact briefly with Abby's face.

'It's all right,' Abby said gently. 'We have no reason to contact him. I understand, then, that you want to terminate the pregnancy?'

'Yes, I have to,' Kyra said, a note of desperation in her voice. 'I…I don't like the idea of…doing that…but I have no choice.' A large tear oozed from beneath the girl's lowered eyelids and she lifted a hand to wipe it away, bending her head, while Abby passed the box of paper tissues that she kept on her desk.

'What you have growing inside you at the moment, Kyra, is not a baby yet,' Abby said gently. 'It's a minute embryo that has the potential to become a baby, very soon, within three months. But right now it is definitely not a baby.'

Taking her time to comfort the girl, explain what would happen next, offer her counselling, and advise her to tell a trusted friend so that she would have someone of her own age to talk to, Abby felt intense compassion. 'There, but for the grace of God, go I.' The familiar adage came to mind, as it so often did in the course of her job. Gradually, the girl seemed to relax and accept the inevitable.

'There's something I have to ask you, Kyra,' Abby said, when all the other facts were down on paper. 'I want you

to consider very carefully before you answer. Is there any
possibility that you could have contacted AIDS?'

'I…don't think so.' Kyra looked frightened, her face
flushed. 'My boyfriend doesn't go with other girls. I'm
pretty sure I'm the only one.'

'Nevertheless, I would like to order an AIDS test, Kyra,
just to eliminate the possibility,' Abby said gently. 'Your
chances of having AIDS are not great, I think, but we do
have to be sure. I will, of course, need your consent.'

'Will it be all right that my…my parents are not told
about the operation? You know…because I'm not eighteen
yet?'

'Yes, it will be all right. For something like this you can
give your own consent to operation once you're sixteen.'

'Good. I was so worried.' The girl relaxed back in the
chair, her relief almost palpable.

Abby did not add that there would be no intimation of
moral judgement. She hoped that she did not need to say
it, that it would be self-evident. Kyra was very frightened,
for so many reasons. Abby would do her best to alleviate
that fear.

They were going to be late for the lecture at the university.
Abby hurried from the elevators to the front lobby several
hours later, where she could see Cheryl waiting for her.

Stuffing the remains of a sandwich into her mouth to
stave off the pangs of hunger, she waved to her friend as
she dodged through incoming patients, their relatives and
milling staff intent on buying snacks for lunch at the coffee-
cart there. She had changed hurriedly into jeans and a loose
sweater. With her long legs and determined stride she was
able to cover the distance in seconds.

'I was just about to leave without you,' Cheryl greeted
her. 'Looks like rain outside, too. Come on. Maybe we'll
make it before the heavens open.'

They headed to the revolving doors to the outside. 'I'm

starving,' Abby said, rushing to keep up with Cheryl who had a head start. 'Positively hypoglycemic. Didn't get any lunch, apart from one measly sandwich.'

'What else is new? Maybe we can pick up a morsel or two at U of G.'

'Oh, damn. It's raining,' Abby sighed, as they emerged into the warm air of late spring.

'Maybe we can beg a ride with someone. Lots of the medical guys go past the campus to get to Gresham General,' Cheryl remarked hopefully. With that, she began to peer into cars that were parked nearby. It was a stopping only, no parking zone.

'Are you looking for a ride?' a familiar deep voice addressed them from the open window of a large gray Buick that had cruised to a halt beside them. Dr Contini thrust his head through the window, appraising both of them, his dark hair falling over his forehead in an almost boyish way as the rain beat down on him.

'We sure are,' Cheryl answered, as quick as a flash, bending down to his level. 'We have to get to the university and we've only got ten minutes to spare.'

'Ah, that's par for the course when you're in the company of Dr Gibson, I believe.' He smiled, shifting his gaze to Abby's flushed face, teasing her. She returned his look with a stony expression. 'I'm on my way to Gresham General. Get in.'

'Are you sure it's no trouble, Dr Contini?' Cheryl asked, gushing a little.

'Quite sure.'

Quickly Abby opened the rear door and got in, so that she would not have to sit up front with Blake. At that moment she felt acutely conscious of him physically, as well as a certain hostility which had sprung from somewhere in her psychic defense system, maybe because it seemed to her that their kisses had not affected him as much as they had affected her. 'Devastated' was the word that came to mind as she contemplated his dark head in front of her. She was certainly in danger of becoming very mixed up.

Cheryl ran round the front of the car to get in beside him. All through the short journey Cheryl prattled on, talking about the lecture they were going to, answering Blake's questions about the family practice program. Once, his amused blue eyes met those of Abby in the rear-view mirror and she looked away hastily, wondering why she felt so discomfited.

After he had dropped them off beside the appropriate lecture hall, Abby realized that she had not uttered one word in the car.

'I've never known you to have verbal diarrhea to quite that extent before, Cheryl,' she said tartly.

'Well, isn't he just gorgeous? He made me nervous.'

'So I observed.'

'You know,' Cheryl said, 'all the time I was talking I had the impression that he didn't hear one word I was saying…that it was you he was concentrating on.'

'Go on!' Abby chided her, wishing it were true. They made a dash through the rain for the *porte-cochère* of the old and impressive building where the lecture was to be held in the faculty of medicine.

'I'm not joking,' Cheryl insisted breathlessly. 'You'd better watch yourself, girl. Before you know where you are you'll be having a hot, panting affair with him. After all, you're about ripe for it, I would say, after all those years of denial. I wouldn't say no to him myself…'

'Dream on!' Abby said, pulling open the heavy door for them to enter. 'You know me. All work and not much play.'

'Precisely,' Cheryl said.

CHAPTER SIX

THE next few days seemed to go by in a flash. Life was generally hectic, bordering on the frantic at times.

On the Friday, Abby went to see Mr Simmons again, to discover that his induction chemotherapy had been put off and was now scheduled to start on the following Monday, to continue over several days.

'Wish me luck,' he said when she went in to check on him.

'Oh, I will…I do,' she assured him.

'Dr Contini told me that the drugs come all ready prepared with the anti-nausea drugs attached to them,' he said, looking at Abby to elaborate. Still attached to his IV lines, with blood, plasma, and other fluids running into his veins, he looked alert and almost normal as he sat out in a chair, with the bags of fluid suspended on metal poles beside it.

'Yes,' she confirmed. 'You get the chemo drugs through an ordinary IV line, like the ones you have now. Then the anti-nausea drugs come in little plastic piggyback bags which are then attached separately to the main IV line, like those antibiotic bags. Then we can adjust the flow of those drugs separately.'

'Sounds as though I'm really going to need those,' he said ruefully.

'Yes. They're pretty effective so don't you worry too much. Well, good luck. I'll be in to see you mid-week, if not sooner.'

When she left the hospital that evening to go home, she thought again of Mr Simmons, who had to spend his week-end waiting and worrying about the forthcoming treatment. Such thoughts made her appreciate the sunshine, the warmth of the evening air, the promises of summer that were all around her, the sounds of birds twittering in the trees near the hospital entrance. It was good to hear the birds against the ever-present sound of city traffic in the background.

That weekend she was going to visit her parents to talk to her father about his new career of growing and marketing organic vegetables and fruit. He had started the business a year and a half ago, after he had been laid off from his long-time office job with the railway. As Abby walked towards the subway station to get her train home, she thought wryly about the awful fear that had descended on her family when that event had taken place. Yet since then her father had said that the change had been the best thing that had happened to him in a very long time.

Out of an enforced change had come a completely new way of life. Abby knew that she owed a lot to her kind, generous parents. One day soon—very soon—she could begin to make it up to them.

When she got home there was an invitation in the mail for her from Blake's office, formally inviting her to his garden party which was to be held on the following Saturday. The RSVP was to be addressed to his secretary. 'I'll go, of course.' Abby said the words aloud. There was no alternative. Even now, her heart leapt with the anticipation of seeing him in a setting outside of the hospital.

All too soon the interlude was over. Abby's thoughts lingered on that lovely, lazy weekend during the following week when her hectic schedule threatened to overwhelm her. Mr Simmons had started his chemo when she went to see him on the Tuesday.

'Hi,' he said weakly, not turning his head, as Abby pressed buttons on the computer beside his bed to read the treatment protocol. It was evident that he felt sick, too sick to chat.

Tim Barrick, the medical resident, came in to join her.

'Hi, Abby,' he said quietly, looking at the screen with her. 'He's getting mitoxantrone and high-dose Ara-C in normal saline,' he explained, naming the anti-leukemic drugs. 'And he's getting the usual cocktail of anti-emetic drugs.'

'I see,' she said. 'How long will all this take, Tim?'

'This time he'll be in hospital for four to six weeks.'

She saw that the photograph of Mr Simmons's wife and children, together with another framed photograph of older children, was positioned on his bedside table in easy view. The sight of those pictures brought a lump to Abby's throat.

For their patient, the images of those people were like a lifeline to the outside world, the normal world of ongoing life. Whenever he opened his eyes to look at them he could remember that lifeline. In a way, they were the equivalent of a child's teddy bear, or the familiar old blanket from home that a child clung to for security.

'Hang in there, Mr Simmons,' Tim Barrick said as the man kept his eyes resolutely closed, fighting nausea.

Not trusting her voice, Abby squeezed his hand, then left the room. Drugs other than the ones she had suggested in her write-up were being used—probably they were the most up to date. She would ask Blake Contini about that. Thinking about him, she realized that she had missed seeing him on the floor.

Her electronic beeper went off as she was leaving the floor so she went back to the nurses' station to call the locating service.

'Dr Gibson, there's a page for you from Dr Blake Contini. He wants you to call him at his office number,' someone at Locating informed her.

'Thanks.' At the sound of his name, her heart had begun its usual accelerated beat, bringing a surge of pleasure. Maybe he would want to quiz her about Mr Simmons's treatment, she speculated, going over in her mind the names and dosages of the drugs he was getting. Then she dialled the number.

'I'm about to visit Dr Ryles,' he informed her instead, 'so I thought that if you were free you would like to come with me.'

'I do have a few minutes,' she said, glad of his invitation. 'And, yes, I would like to see him. I've yet to see him awake since he was admitted. I've just been to see Mr Simmons...I'm on the floor.'

'Come round to my office, then,' he invited. 'I've looked over the notes you made—they were good. The chemotherapy drugs were different, that's all. We can discuss that later also.'

'All right. Thank you.'

He met her in the corridor and together they went to the coronary care unit. Although they made conversation on the way, Abby was conscious of a certain tension that she could not place. One thing she was sure of—it was not all coming from her.

'So you're Dr Gibson.' Will Ryles said, by way of greeting. He was sitting in a comfortable chair beside his bed in a private room that was part of the ambulatory section of the coronary care unit. He grasped Abby's extended hand firmly. 'At long last I get to meet you.'

The smile that he gave her lit up his pale face...a face that still betrayed a chronic tiredness, but not as badly as it had done when she had first set eyes on him in the basement corridor.

'Very pleased to meet you.' Abby smiled back. 'Glad to see you're up.'

'It seems that I owe my life to your prompt reaction, Dr Gibson. Thank you. It's good to be alive after all. There were a few times when I wondered... There's nothing like a brush with your actual demise to help you get your priorities sorted out.'

'Hope you're not concerning yourself too much with hospital politics while you're in here, Will. Let someone else worry about it,' Blake cut in smoothly, sensing that she was not used to being put on the spot like that. With a small, sideways smile, Abby let him know that she appreciated him taking over the situation.

'I haven't given up, Blake,' Dr Ryles said. 'Ginny is doing some of the detective work for me. It's not change I object to, as such—that has to come at some point. It's just that there are so many vested interests in private medical care, muscling in on hospital budgets, public money raised from taxes…It's borderline fraud. And I'm going to expose it if I can.'

Blake put a hand on the older man's shoulder. 'Yes, and I'm going to help, Will. Leave it to me and the other guys. While you're in here, for goodness' sake, relax, man! You're no good to anyone if you're sick,' Blake cajoled him. 'I'm making progress with my detective work, too. Ginny's like a terrier with a rat…If there's anything underhand going on, she'll find it.'

Dr Ryles chuckled. 'Too true,' he agreed.

'I'll see you tomorrow, Will,' Blake said, getting ready to leave. 'Read a few detective stories, watch some television—anything to take your mind off the radiology department. Ok?'

'Sure.' Dr Ryles managed to raise a smile.

Out in the corridor, Abby and Blake stood together for a few minutes.

'He looks much better, Dr Contini,' Abby ventured.

'Yes, he's going to be all right. He just needs a good, long rest. He's not the sort of man to take a rest voluntarily. Several of us are working on that too—to have him go up to a cottage by a lake when he gets out of here.'

'That's a great idea.' Abby smiled, thinking of lakes in 'cottage country', about a two-hour drive from Gresham. 'I think we could all do with a little of that treatment right now.'

'Do you have a cottage?' he asked.

'Oh, no…no.'

'To change the subject, I hope you'll be at my garden party on Saturday.' He took a step back, as though distancing himself from her—as though his mind was already on work he had to do. Today he wore his white lab coat over a formal dark grey suit and striped shirt that looked as though they had been made for him.

'Yes, I will,' she agreed. 'I'm looking forward to it.'

'Well, goodbye, Abby. See you then.' He smiled slightly, only a certain light in his eyes giving away any indication that he thought of the interlude of passion that they had shared, while she knew that her cheeks were tinged with a faint colour. 'I've invited at least one other resident so you won't feel on your own, I hope. Some people your own age.'

As he strode away from her, she stood, watching, until he was out of sight. By that last remark he had inadvertently put her in another category from himself—one of the younger medical generation—although she doubted that he was more than about eight years older than she was. On second thoughts, perhaps it had been deliberate. And by that he had somehow distanced himself from her. Was it because he was married? None of the usual gossips seemed to know.

There was an unfamiliar ache in her heart as she walked away, a longing for something that she could not put a name to. She forced her thoughts ahead to all she had to get through before the end of the day.

Both she and Cheryl had to be at Gresham General on the Thursday of that week to check on some patients of the senior GPs with whom they worked who admitted patients to both hospitals.

They shared a third friend's old car for the journey, a distance of about a mile and a half from University Hospital, still in the downtown area of Gresham. The day was bright and clear, the wide main streets busy with traffic. Abby wore a light jacket over her usual neat blouse and skirt.

'Ah…it's great to have a change of scene for a while,' Abby said, enjoying the warm breeze blowing through the interior of the car that tumbled her soft hair into disarray.

'What do you have to do at the General?' Cheryl asked.

'I have two patients to see in the chronic care unit. Both had strokes and ended up there because they don't have close families who can look after them. They're Dr Wharton's patients. He wants me to review their medications and their progress. Hopefully, both of them will eventually go home, then come several times a week to the day centre for physiotherapy and occupational therapy.'

'Dr Wharton's not such an old fuddy-duddy as he first seems,' Cheryl commented. 'He's pretty shrewd really. Yet when I first met him, in all my youthful arrogance, I thought he ought to have retired long ago. Now I can see that he only seems slow because he's very thoughtful, careful and thorough about all that he does.'

'Yes. He's not the sort of man you would catch making a mistake,' Abby said. 'Who are you seeing?'

'One of our patients was admitted there last night as an emergency—someone from our diabetic clinic—in a coma. She's a bit of a problem because she doesn't test her blood sugar before eating.'

'A rebel?'

'You could say that. She's young… It's depressing when you can't lead a normal life.'

The three parted at the main entrance to the hospital, from where Abby made her way to the chronic care unit, which was a relatively new add-on to an older building.

Once there, she took a flight of stairs to the second floor. The two women she had to see were in the same room.

Oddly enough, they were both unmarried women in their early sixties, although from very different backgrounds, who had no close family members. Since being in this hospital they had struck up a friendship of sorts, born of their rather desperate mutual need. Abby hoped to encourage this by persuading them to attend the day unit once they were discharged. She thought of the old saying that necessity made strange bedfellows, or something like that...

A nurse came out of a room quickly and almost careened into Abby as she walked briskly along the corridor of the unit on the second floor. 'Oh, sorry...' the nurse said, stopping to look at Abby. There was an expression of intense anxiety on her face, a frowning concentration, that caught Abby's attention instantly. 'Are you Dr Gibson?' the nurse added breathlessly.

'Yes, I am.'

'Could you help me, please? I've got an awful problem. Come into this room.'

'Yes. What is it?' Following the nurse into the room, Abby could see that it was occupied by only one patient, who lay perfectly still in the high bed. A very pale face, surrounded by long blonde hair, female, young—those were the things that registered instantly on her mind as she surveyed the room quickly.

Hastily the nurse closed the door behind them. 'She's in respiratory arrest,' the nurse said urgently. 'Her lungs are full of mucus. She suddenly stopped breathing just a moment ago. I've had the suction going for the last little while, but I can't get her started. Her heart's still going...'

At the bedside, Abby felt for the woman's carotid pulse, noting the pale, porcelain-like features as she did so. This woman was young—about thirty, it seemed—thin and almost childlike. The eyes were closed, her lips slack, yet there was a delicate beauty about her that was strangely poignant.

'She's been in a coma for over a year,' the nurse explained hurriedly. 'She was in an accident, received brain damage, never regained consciousness after that. I...I was just about to intubate her...I have the intubation tray here, with all the necessary equipment. But...um...I don't know...'

'Why isn't she on a ventilator?'

'She's been breathing by herself, although she's had some low-grade chest infections over the year.'

When Abby looked at the nurse's face, hearing the tremor in her voice, she saw that her eyes were full of tears.

'Why didn't you intubate her?' she asked, 'You know how to, I assume?'

'Oh, yes.' The nurse was distraught. 'You see, she's a ''no-code''—not to be resuscitated. Although this isn't exactly a situation for a cardiac arrest code yet, she'll arrest if I don't get her breathing again, won't she!'

'Yes...' Abby considered the difference between a cardiac arrest, where the heart suddenly stopped, and respiratory arrest, where there was usually a mechanical reason why a patient stopped breathing—lungs full of mucus, or swelling in the airway that blocked the intake of air.

The nurse took hold of Abby's arm urgently. 'I can't do it. I can't just let her die. I've been her nurse since she was admitted to this unit.' Tears ran down her cheeks. 'And I'm a Catholic... It's against all that I believe in, to let her die like this when there's a chance of saving her. She...she's only thirty years old...'

While the nurse had been explaining the situation, Abby had checked out the equipment that was in the room—the piped oxygen and built-in suction apparatus which were standard in any room like this, the intubation tray, which had been opened up from its sterile wrappings on the bedside table.

It took seconds only to size up the situation. Abby made a decision. 'You have a flexible bronchoscope on this floor, I assume?' she said. The bronchoscope was a long, thin fibre-optic tube, connected to a powerful light source, that could be inserted via the throat down the trachea into the lungs, enabling the doctor to look deep into the airway to find out what was causing the blockage.

'Yes. I…I was just going to get that. I think we should just go ahead and do it…try to save her.'

'Run and get it—quickly. I'll intubate her. I want the bronchoscope in case I can't get the tube in,' Abby said tersely, selecting a 6.5 endotracheal tube from the tray, together with the laryngoscope. 'In any case, I'll want to have a look-see down her trachea and into the bronchus…suck out some of that mucus.'

'Thank you…thank you.' There was a muffled sob in the nurse's voice as she headed towards the door. 'I can't just let her die. I can't…'

'Please bring one of the portable ventilators as well when you've done that,' Abby called after her. 'I'll bag her manually until you get it.'

'Yes, I will. And be careful, Dr Gibson. She's HIV-positive.' With that, the nurse was out of the room, leaving the door slightly open, then she was running down the corridor.

Abby checked the pulse again. It was still there, shallow but unmistakable. As she felt it, she thought again of Will Ryles. A woman of this age would have a good, strong heart, but if she didn't get oxygen soon the heart would stop and she would die.

In the pocket of her lab coat Abby always carried a pair of clear plastic goggles to protect her eyes from splashes of blood or any other body fluids from HIV positive patients. Automatically, she pulled them out and put them on, then put on a pair of sterile latex gloves that were in the tray.

Yes, there was thick mucus in the patient's throat; it was clearly visible with the bright light from the laryngoscope when Abby had it in place. Maybe there was an incipient pneumonia, common in patients who had been in a coma for a long time.

Working quickly, she suctioned out as much of it as she could, then deftly inserted the endotracheal tube which she had lubricated with Xylocaine gel. With a long, thin plastic tube attached to the wider suction tubing, she probed through the endotracheal tube into the bronchus.

There was something very satisfying about clearing out a patient's airway, Abby conceded as the mucus disappeared into the suction catheter and thence to a plastic waste disposal bag. As the airway cleared, the woman's chest began to move slightly as she made motions to breathe, but they were scarcely strong enough.

'Ok, that's enough.' Abby spoke aloud to herself. 'Get the oxygen in.'

There was piped oxygen in the room, with a flow gauge attached to the wall. With practiced skill, Abby connected the newly inserted endotracheal tube to a rubber bag which she would compress to force the gas into the patient's lungs, and this to the tube providing the supply of oxygen.

The nurse was back, taking in at a glance the state of affairs as she rushed to set up the bronchoscope with the efficiency of an expert. Once connected to a light source, they would use it to suck out more of the obstructing mucus.

'Thank God you've got her intubated, Dr Gibson,' the nurse said. 'Thank you. I'll think about the consequences later. Do you think she'll breathe spontaneously in a while? I do hope so. Otherwise…' She left the sentence unfinished, hanging in the air like a dark, ominous cloud, as Abby pressed the rubber bag manually to force oxygen down into the lungs.

'She was making the motions a moment ago,' Abby said,

'but I'm going to put her on the ventilator anyway, to be on the safe side.' The mechanical ventilator would take over the breathing function, ensuring that the chest expanded and relaxed at regular intervals, pushing oxygen into the lungs.

They both knew that the patient's problem might have more to do with her brain damage, a deteriorating condition, as much as from mucus obstructing her airway.

'I'll get the ventilator set up,' the nurse added.

'I may be in a better position to answer your question when I've had a look at her chart and her medical history,' Abby said succinctly, her mind buzzing with possibilities for keeping this young woman alive.

Those consequences, of which the nurse had spoken, came soon enough in the shape of the senior medical resident, who arrived on the floor to do a routine check of his patients just as Abby went into the office on the unit to look for the chart of the woman, filed under the room number. In her frantic haste she had not learned the name of the patient.

Just as she found the appropriate chart, the medical resident came into the office, a set expression on his face.

'Didn't you know that patient was a no-code?' he demanded quietly, so that no ambulatory patients could possibly hear him. 'Why have you got her intubated and on a respirator? She's not even your patient.'

'Yes, I was told she was a no-code,' Abby replied tersely, sizing him up, while she flipped open the chart at page one. 'It wasn't a question of a code, anyway. She didn't have a cardiac arrest. We got her in time…she simply stopped breathing. She was obstructed.'

Striving not to feel defensive in the face of his obvious chagrin, Abby decided not to try to justify her action to him, other than to add, 'I'm not in the habit of just standing by while a patient dies when there's something I can do to prevent it.'

He gave her a penetrating look. 'It's a pretty messy case,' he said. 'She's HIV-positive as well.'

'The nurse told me that, too,' Abby said abruptly. 'There's no guarantee that she'll start breathing on her own again, is there? So then you—or whoever decided on the no-code—can have the satisfaction of turning off the ventilator, can't you?'

His quick frown told her that maybe she had gone too far.

'Look...' he began.

Holding up a hand, Abby stopped him. 'All right... Sorry,' she said. 'Sorry. I'm a little emotional right now. It'll pass.'

When he shrugged and held out a hand to her, she took it.

'I'm sorry, too,' he said. 'But I think it's pretty hopeless. I'm Stewart Hadley, by the way.'

'Abby Gibson.'

'Hi,' he added, unbending a little. A year or two older than she was herself, he had the usual tired, overworked look about him.

'Read the chart anyway,' he offered. 'You might find it interesting.'

'I'll write up what I did, even though she's not my patient,' she said, 'so there's a record of it.'

'Sure,' he said.

There was no one else in the office, so when he left she sat down at one end of the big desk there and opened the file.

A sense of shock, like a dousing of very cold water, passed over her as she saw the patient's name. Numbly she stared at it for what seemed like long minutes. 'Kaitlin Amanda Contini...' she read. The typed words seemed to jump out at her. Her eyes skimmed down the 'face sheet' at the beginning of the file, looking for the name of the next of kin. Yes, there it was—'Blake Contini, husband.'

'Oh, my God!'

Abby did not read any more, feeling uncomfortably as though she were invading the privacy of the Contini family, but simply took a clean medical note sheet from the desk and began to write.

Dr Hadley was right, of course—she was not the woman's doctor. A check on the face-sheet again, which gave all the basic information about a patient, showed her that the woman was under the care of one of the neurologists in the hospital, plus several other senior doctors who were in consultation with each other.

With meticulous care and accuracy, rigidly holding her feelings in check, she recorded everything that she had done for Kaitlin Amanda Contini, first including the part where she had been asked for help by the nurse. Having done that, she turned to the medication order sheet and prescribed a broad-spectrum antibiotic for the woman, to be given initially as a stat IV bolus, to be followed by intramuscular injections at regular intervals for ten days. Then she typed the orders into the computer.

From the medication sheet, it looked as though there was not much active treatment going on, in spite of the impressive medical team that was taking care of her—at least on paper. The reality was probably that the senior residents of the medical and neurology departments did the day-to-day work of caring for her, plus her nurse.

'I'll be damned if I'll just walk away!' Abby muttered to herself. 'I'm going to finish the job—and do it properly.' Before leaving the floor, she would tell the same nurse that she had written up some stat antibiotics for Mrs Contini. She knew that the very competent nurse would give them right away.

Mrs Contini! The name pulled her up short again with a peculiar sense of dissonance. How odd that name sounded.

It was one day less than a fortnight since Abby had met Dr Blake Contini, yet there was a feeling that she had known him for much longer. Now she thought she could see why he had kissed her with such desperate hunger, and why he had initially held back.

What did it matter to her, Abby, personally that he was married? That he had a wife who was desperately ill? But it *did* matter. For reasons that she could not entirely fathom, it mattered very much. Maybe it was nothing more than the pull of a strong physical attraction, coupled with her own sublimated needs…

Abby closed her eyes, pressing her fingers against her eyelids. Fatigue weighed her down like a physical load, made more noticeable after the sudden surge of adrenalin that had coursed through her body earlier during the unexpected emergency which, as things went in acute hospitals, had been no big deal. Yet this was the chronic care unit; that in itself always held a terrible poignancy, when a young person had to be consigned to a chronic care unit because there was little or no hope that they could resume a normal life…

After returning the chart to its slot, she returned to Mrs Contini's room. The nurse, who was with Stewart Hadley, saw her hovering at the door and came over. Quietly, Abby told her of the medication she had ordered.

The nurse nodded, smiling. 'I'll make sure she gets it right away. Thank you for what you did,' she said quietly. 'Will I see you on the floor later? Dr Wharton's two patients?'

'Yes. I'm going to get a quick coffee now, down in the lobby. Um…has anyone called Dr Contini—her husband?' How odd that sounded, especially coming from her own lips. In truth, she was desperate to get away for a while to think.

'I've just called him,' the nurse confirmed. 'He's coming over here from University Hospital. He must be on his way now.'

Abby left the floor, feeling like an automaton. She had to get out.

CHAPTER SEVEN

AFTER buying a cup of coffee from the little coffee-shop off the front lobby of the hospital, Abby went to sit on a bench on a patch of grass in front of the building, shaded by a tree from the early summer sun. The face of Kaitlin Contini stayed in her mind as she sipped the coffee. Imagine being in a coma for over a year, she thought consideringly. Totally out of it. The thought was sobering to an unbearable degree. At least you wouldn't know about the deterioration of your body…

Stewart Hadley was walking over the grass towards her when she looked up. He was tall and gangly, with an awkwardness about him that was almost adolescent. His white lab coat was flapping open, his pockets stuffed with the paraphernalia of his job.

'The nurse said I would find you here.' He sat down carefully beside her, balancing the Styrofoam cup of coffee that he had brought with him. 'I want to apologize for my brusqueness earlier. Megan—that's the nurse up there— bawled me out about it.' He took a slug of the coffee, swilling it around in his mouth before swallowing. 'Ah, that's good…for a guy who's been up most of the night and didn't get any breakfast.'

Abby grinned. 'Apology accepted,' she said.

'You probably didn't get time to read the case history,' he said.

'No. I was going to. Then I saw that she's the wife of Blake Contini. It was a shock. You see, I work with him…don't know him very well…' Abby explained how she felt about not wanting to invade their privacy.

'Yeah,' Stewart said, 'I see what you mean. Abby…I

saw her when she first came in here. I don't mind admitting that I think it's time for her to let go. It sounds awful—my heart bleeds for her—but she's deteriorated so much. There's no hope. We have to be realistic. The family decided on a no-code about two weeks ago. It was hard for them. She has two kids.'

'What happened, Stewart?' Abby asked quietly.

'To cut a long story short, she had a long-standing affair with another man, who was probably the one who gave her AIDS. They went to Jamaica together for a holiday and had a boating accident. He is—or was, more like it—some sort of rich playboy, apparently. He escaped with minor injuries while she was thrown from the boat and hit her head, the result being the coma which she never came out of.'

'Oh, God,' Abby murmured, feeling physically sick. 'How awful. Were they…were she and Dr Contini separated then?'

'No, they were still married, as far as I know. I told you it was messy, didn't I? And I mean in more ways than one. It gets worse. She also broke both legs and injured her spine. She's paralyzed from the waist down.'

'I had no idea. Of course, Dr Contini's only been at University Hospital a short time. I suppose it's only a matter of time before it will be common knowledge.'

'You bet,' Stewart said grimly. 'It's only because of excellent nursing care that she's still alive, that she hasn't got pressure sores all over her body. It was while she was in hospital in Jamaica after the accident that they discovered she was HIV positive.' He took another swallow of coffee. 'To cap it all, the guy she was with is also in this hospital. His name's Todd Braxton. He's got full-blown AIDS, and is in a bad way.'

Leaning back against the seat, Abby groaned. 'Anything else?'

'Yeah. I shouldn't think he'll last much longer. He's in the palliative care unit. The really pathetic thing about it all is that he can still walk about a bit. He goes from his floor to see her every day… He sits holding her hand, crying.' Stewart swallowed more coffee. 'He loves her, you see. Poor sod, he feels guilty.'

'Should he feel guilty?'

'I reckon he should, because word has it that he caused the accident. I expect he's crying for himself as well as for her. Sitting there, holding her hand, gives him a bit of comfort, assuages his guilt, even if she'll never know he was there.'

'Oh, Stewart, I feel like having a good cry myself. You're right about it being a mess.' Her voice shook with emotion.

'You can cry if you like, Abby…so long as you let me kiss you better.' Stewart's attempt at a joke fell rather flat but, nonetheless, Abby felt herself warming towards him.

'You have to keep a sense of perspective, Abby, to keep yourself sane,' Stewart went on, staring across the sunlit patch of grass. 'We have done, and are doing, all we can… That's what I keep on reminding myself of.'

'Yes, I know, Stewart,' she said quietly. 'You must have done a great job, too, to keep her going this long. Friends?' Abby extended a hand to him. Awkwardly he took it, then put his arm around her shoulders in a quick hug.

'Yeah, sure,' he said. 'Keep your sense of humour, Abby, and you'll be all right.'

'I could sure use a few hugs, Stewart. These last two weeks have been rather stressful in one way and another,' she said. 'Um…what about Blake, Kaitlin's husband? And her children?'

'They come to see her regularly. They cry too. At least, the kids do. He just looks bloody awful,' Stewart Hadley said matter-of-factly, although Abby knew now that he cared very much. 'Maybe it's better to just let her go…But I think the kids like to know that she's there, to see her…'

'Yes…of course they do,' Abby agreed softly, trying to

picture Blake's children. 'How old are they?' She hadn't wanted to think of him as married, least of all to be a father. That in itself was a revelation of sorts. A sobering personal disappointment superimposed itself on the tragedy of the situation to which there was no good solution.

'About ten, I think. Twin boys. It's a real dilemma, but one that becomes more clear-cut every day, I think. At least, to me it does. We get a lot of stories similar to that in here. It's just life—there's nothing that's really unique.' Stewart Hadley had a world-weary air, sobering in one so young, as though he had seen it all, if not done it all.

'Thank you for telling me, Stewart. I appreciate it, and I apologize, too, if I seemed a little holier-than-thou up there in the unit,' Abby said, touching his arm commiseratingly.

'It's ok,' he said. 'I understand how you feel. I haven't got so hard-boiled that I can't understand that.'

'Thanks for seeing it that way.' Abby smiled.

'Going back up to the unit, Abby?' He stood up. 'Break over?'

'Yes.'

'I'll walk with you.'

'I have to see two other patients up there,' Abby said.

'Hey...talk of the devil...' He stopped when they were halfway back to the entrance as a large gray Buick, familiar to Abby, went by at speed towards one of the many small hospital car parks. 'That's Dr Contini. Someone must have called him, told him his wife had almost died.'

'Yes, that's his car.' Abby's heart had given an uncomfortable lurch of recognition. 'The nurse called him.' Apprehension mingled oddly with a reluctant acknowledgement that she wanted to see him again when she considered that she might bump into him on the unit.

Maybe it would be better to avoid him if she could do so. It was an odd situation—maybe he would not have wanted her to make sure that his wife could breathe. A strong sense of empathy for his situation, as well as for his wife, made her vulnerable.

'Maybe I'd better have a few words with him,' Dr Hadley said, reluctance in his stance. 'Not something I look forward to.'

'I…don't particularly want to meet up with him,' Abby said, walking beside her colleague.

'You seeing those two lovely ladies with the strokes? What characters, eh? I love going to see 'em myself…sure makes a change.'

'The very ones,' Abby agreed, trying to tear her thoughts away from Blake Contini, from the brief image of his set face that she had caught a glimpse of as he had driven past.

Their conversation was interrupted by the shrill 'beep-beep' of Stewart Hadley's electronic pager which he kept clipped to the upper pocket of his lab coat. As he checked it, they both looked at the number that was displayed on the tiny computerized display screen.

'Damn!' Stewart said. 'It's the chronic care unit. Maybe there's a code. I'd better get up there. See you, Abby.' He set off at a loping walk that was almost a run, while Abby followed slowly, oddly reluctant to go up again to the unit.

She had a premonition that something had happened to Kaitlin Contini. If that was the case, she would keep well out of it. She was not, after all, on the staff of the Gresham General.

Once back on the unit, Abby decided to head for the female staff washroom, stalling a bit for time, not ready to face Blake Contini. Also, she wanted to be in a more apparently optimistic frame of mind when she went to see the two stroke patients.

As she rounded a corner of a corridor she saw activity around the entrance to Kaitlin Contini's room, and her heart seemed to drop. Staff doctors were heading there and others were going in and out, as well as several nurses. Megan, the nurse she had assisted earlier, hurried up to the room, pushing the portable cardiac defibrillator, and disappeared with it inside.

It was clear to Abby that the woman had suffered a cardiac arrest and, although she was a no-code, the staff members were trying to resuscitate her…maybe because Blake was there.

Abby went into the washroom quickly, feeling physically sick again. There was something especially tragic about the death of a young woman…if that was happening. Her intuition, based on experience, plus the evidence before her, told her that it was… There was an odd feeling that a halt, too, had been called on something she had begun to hope for, something that had been given barely enough time to take shape.

As she applied a little make-up to her face, she stared at her own reflection and knew that she had begun to have an idea, vague though it might be, that Dr Contini could mean something to her in a personal way…and she to him. Now it seemed like a madness, a delusion. Yet there had been something between them…surely?

The young woman in the bed, looking like a snow princess in a child's fairy-tale, had once lived a normal life—had run and danced, walked on beaches in warm surf, held her babies in her arms. Had she once loved Blake? Clearly something had gone wrong.

'Dr Gibson!' The voice that addressed her as she made her exit from the washroom was clearly recognizable.

There was no escaping him. He was right there in the corridor, coming towards her, as the activity around Mrs Contini's room remained undiminished. His face was ashen as he reached her and took her arm to detain her. With a movement of his head, he indicated that they should go into an unoccupied room.

'What happened here?' he said harshly when they were inside. 'My wife's nurse told me that you helped to intubate

her, put her on a ventilator. How come you got involved—
a family practice doctor-in-training?'

There was something accusatory about his tone, about
his pale, frowning regard, that made Abby cringe away
from him mentally. The expression in his eyes was distant,
glazed with grief.

'I was on the unit to see two of Dr Wharton's patients,'
Abby began, feeling chilled by the way he was looking at
her, as though he hardly saw her as a human being, only
as some sort of instrument who might have, in some way
contributed to his wife's death. 'It was an emergency.'

Keeping to the point, she outlined what had happened.
'She...she was all right when I left the unit,' she ended.

'Well, she had a cardiac arrest shortly after that,' he said.
'I was in my car, going to the university, when I got a call
on my car phone, so I came straight here. Is there anything
you could have done to precipitate this?'

Although the words were spoken levelly, Abby, sensitive
to nuances, was aware of an underlying insinuation that
perhaps she had been negligent. 'No,' she said bluntly. 'I
did everything I could to prevent it. I've written down in
the chart everything I did, Dr Contini, if you care to look
at it. How is she?'

'Not good.' The bleakness in his words was chilling. Any
rapport that they had previously built up had apparently
dissipated.

'I...I'm so sorry.' She stumbled over the words. 'She
was a no-code, I understand...' Surely he would have been
the one, as the husband, to have made the decision to have
that sort of medical status for his wife. 'It looks as though
a code was called after all.'

'Yes,' he said savagely. 'When it comes to the crunch,
you can't do it...can't just let them go without making an
effort...not when someone's as young as Kaitlin.'

'No. That's why I put her on a ventilator when she
stopped breathing. I'm so sorry.' Tears were forming in her

eyes, much as she tried to stop them. She wanted to comfort him, yet there was no way.

'I thought maybe you did something to precipitate this…' he said.

'I don't see how. All I did was suction out mucus, give oxygen, intubate her, then put her on the ventilator. I ordered no drugs, other than antibiotics.' Feeling like ice, numb with shock that he might think her incompetent, Abby leaned against a desk. 'She was on a monitor, of course… Her heart rate and blood pressure were within normal limits when I left her, the oxygen uptake was ok and Dr Hadley, the senior resident, was there also when I left.'

'Hmm.' He began to pace up and down the small room. From time to time he ran a hand distractedly through his hair. 'I'm trying to get a picture of what might have happened. By the time I got here they were trying to get her heart going. I know it was just a matter of time… I should be prepared for this, but I'm not…'

Someone came through the door, a senior consultant by the look of him, and closed the door quietly behind him. With a quick glance at Abby, noting her lab coat with a stethoscope stuffed in the pocket, he obviously decided he could speak in front of her.

'I'm afraid she's gone, Blake,' the doctor said quietly. 'We did what we could. Looks like a pulmonary embolism to me, for her to go as quickly as that. I'm sorry, but probably this is the best way. She couldn't have known anything about it.'

'No…no.' Blake Contini said the words automatically, as he briefly closed his eyes and passed a hand over his face.

Abby wanted to run to him, to comfort him. Instead, she stood stiffly, feeling in the way, wishing she could become invisible.

A pulmonary embolism—a blood clot in the pulmonary

artery in the lungs—killed quickly, she knew. When a patient spent a long time in bed, as did those in comas—as Kaitlin Contini had done—clots formed in the veins in the legs and sometimes a piece of a clot broke off and travelled to the lungs, causing instant death from blockage of a vital blood vessel. Yes, that would most likely be the explanation…

She needn't have worried about being in the way. The two men left the room without a backward glance.

'Would you like to see her, Blake?' the other man said as they went out, putting an arm briefly on Blake's shoulder as though to help him from the room.

'Yes.'

Resisting the urge to weep, with all the will-power at her disposal Abby composed herself as best she could, and had almost succeeded when Megan burst into the room.

'Ah, Dr Gibson.' She came forward. 'There's a message for you from Dr Wharton's office. They want to know if you've seen his two patients yet. I said you were with them right now so maybe he wants you back at University Hospital.' There was evidence that the nurse had been crying.

'Thanks. I'll go to see them right now.'

'She died, you know,' Megan said quietly, a catch in her voice. 'I've looked after her since she came in…Dr Hadley and myself.'

'Yes.'

'It's going to seem strange without her…real strange. I want to thank you again for what you did, Dr Gibson. It was most likely a pulmonary embolism that got her.'

'There was nothing more anyone could have done, Megan,' Abby said gently. 'It's a tribute to your good nursing, and to the rest of the team, that she lasted this long.'

The nurse nodded. 'All the same,' she whispered, 'you know how it is.'

Abby did know. 'Dr Contini seems to think I might have precipitated her cardiac arrest,' she said.

'I've just given him the chart to read,' the nurse said. 'I've told him how you helped me before I got a chance to call anyone else. He needs something to do, to feel he's doing something useful.'

'I'll go to see those other patients,' Abby said.

Out in the corridor, someone called her. 'Hey…Abby!'

It was Stewart Hadley who was accosting her from down the corridor just as she was steeling herself to enter the office at the nursing station to get the charts of the two patients she had to see. Dr Contini was in the office with one of the other staff men, no doubt going over his wife's medical chart.

When Dr Hadley reached her, seeing her stricken face, he put his arms round her in a quick hug, and she returned the gesture, aware that the two doctors in the office could see them.

'I know how you feel,' he said. 'You don't have to say anything.'

Abby nodded dumbly.

'You expect something,' he continued quietly, 'but you're seldom prepared for it…'

'No…' she said.

'"The awful finality" and all that,' he murmured. 'It really does take you by surprise.'

'I didn't know her…but she was so young…she looked like a girl.'

'Yeah.' He touched her arm. 'You did a great job, you know, Abby.'

'Was it an embolism, do you think?'

'Almost certainly, I would say. They'll do an autopsy.'

'Dr Contini seems to think that my attempt to resuscitate her might have precipitated this.' She whispered the words, looking at Stewart Hadley agonizingly.

'He actually said that? I don't see how it could. Poor

devil… He's just looking for reasons…like we all do. I think she's been deteriorating for several days.' Stewart said quietly, reasonably. 'This was inevitable. Don't let it get to you.'

'I just hope he doesn't blame me somehow…'

'He'll come round,' Stewart said kindly. 'You can feel sorry for me if you like, Abby, since I guess it will fall to my lot to tell Todd Braxton that she's dead. It'll just about finish him off, I should think.'

'Oh, Stewart.' She managed a commiserating smile, 'I certainly don't envy you.'

With another quick hug, he signalled his departure. 'Must go. See you around, Abby.'

'I hope so. Thanks, Stewart.'

As she disentangled herself from his quick embrace, fighting the urge to cry, she glanced towards the office. Blake Contini was standing in the doorway, looking at her. His pale face was blank with grief.

If the two stroke patients noticed a change in Abby since her last visit to them, they were not in a position to comment on it, for which she was grateful. Distracted, she made a supreme effort to pull herself together.

The two women, Rona Duff and Margaret Hamilton, were both sitting out of their respective beds in their shared room when Abby entered.

'Good morning, ladies,' she said, trying to inject some cheer into her voice but feeling the incongruity of it.

They both made a sound that was a good approximation of 'good morning', considering how much their speech had been affected. Their combined effort cheered Abby somewhat. One must be thankful for the checks and balances, the compensations, in life, she reminded herself.

They beamed at Abby, clearly very pleased to have a visitor.

'Dr Wharton asked me to see you,' she explained, 'to

assess your progress. I see your writing has improved. That's really great!' In truth, she still couldn't read it.

Margaret Hamilton made a sound that Abby interpreted as, 'Oh, yes.'

Both women were right handed and because of the hemiplegia, paralysis of the right side of the body, had had to learn to write with their left hands temporarily. They had both tackled the challenge and now spent a great deal of time writing notes to each other, carrying on a written conversation.

Ms Hamilton was a university professor, a teacher in Sociology, who had been still active before her stroke at the University of Gresham, while Rona Duff had worked all her adult life selling women's fashions at a department store in the city. They were an unlikely pair, yet they seemed to complement each other perfectly.

They both had a sense of humour, though of somewhat different types, that enabled them to see the irony and humour in their situation of partial helplessness. There was good reason to hope that they would both recover well.

I'm going to enjoy this, Abby told herself decisively, determined to concentrate on something other than the awful dilemma that had been presented by the condition of Kaitlin Contini.

Nevertheless, as she sat down near the two women, taking out a pad of paper from her bag, she noted that her hands were trembling.

'Now,' she said out loud, swallowing to dispel a constriction in her throat, 'I'm going to ask you some questions about progress before I give you each a physical examination. We'll understand each other as best we can.'

Inwardly, the turmoil continued. Blake... His name seemed to pound in her brain... I'm sorry, so sorry...

It was late when Abby got home that evening. Desperate to get out of the hospital, to unwind before going home, she had gone to a restaurant by herself for a quick, simple meal. Then all through the journey home she had tried, unsuccessfully, to get the image of Blake's face from her mind. He haunted her, and she wondered how she was going to sleep.

It was silly to feel so involved; after all, she had known him only a short time. Yet she *was* involved. Now she wanted nothing more than a long, relaxing bath in scented water, one of the few, inexpensive indulgences she allowed herself.

Later, after the bath, dressed cosily in dressing-gown and slippers, she was surprised when her intercom buzzed, indicating that someone was down in the lobby pressing her doorbell. Usually, friends and family telephoned before they came round.

'Hello, this is Blake Contini,' the familiar voice said as she answered the buzz by lifting the receiver of the intercom, as though she had conjured the reality of him out of her tortured thoughts. His voice sent her heart rate clamouring as she was beset by a surge of mixed emotions, not least an apprehension that he still somehow held her culpable in his wife's death.

'Oh, hello,' she answered, unable to conceal her surprise.

'I was in the area,' he went on, 'so I decided to drop in on you, if you don't mind. There's something I'd like to say. I hope it isn't inconvenient.'

'Well…' Abby cleared her throat, conscious of being inappropriately attired. 'Just a little. But, please, come up anyway, Dr Contini. I think perhaps we do need to talk.'

'Thank you.' There was, she thought, a certain relief in his voice.

Deciding not to rush to change before he got there, she waited for him by the door.

'I apologize for the intrusion,' he said, eyeing her dressing-gown. 'I had to come.' He was casually dressed himself, as though he had flung on the first clothes that had come to hand, a sharp contrast from the formal, neat suits that he wore at the hospital.

'It's all right. Really,' she reassured him. 'I hope I didn't sound rude. Please, come in and sit down. I'll just change.'

Without a backward glance, she almost fled to her bedroom to put on trousers and a comfortable sweatshirt, hoping that he had been too concerned with his own difficulties to take much note of her blush of pleasure at the sight of him. Nonetheless, she was nervous. Why on earth would he be here except to talk about Kaitlin? Just as well to get it over with now.

'Would you like some hot chocolate?' she asked as she emerged into the sitting room, to find him ensconced on her sofa. 'I intended to make some for myself as it's a cool evening.' The mundane offer helped to diffuse an air of tension.

'That would be nice.' His voice was flat, devoid of emotion. 'Thanks.'

In the kitchen, Abby busied herself heating milk. It was evident that he was still in a state of shock and grief; he seemed to be speaking and acting automatically, as though his mind were elsewhere. Empathy flooded her and made her distracted and clumsy as she poured the milk, spilling a little. Forcing herself to slow down, she began to do everything very deliberately.

'I came here principally to apologize,' he said, as soon as she put down the tray in front of him. 'Such apologies are better said in person. I'm sorry for implying that you might have contributed to Kaitlin's death—it was stupid of me to suggest it.'

Abby decided to remain silent, as she passed him a mug of hot chocolate, not wanting to let him get a hint of how upset she had been by his implication.

'I hope you won't hold it against me, Abby,' he said.

Not trusting her voice, she just shook her head.

'They've already done an autopsy,' he continued. 'They

found multiple emboli in the pulmonary system, which were the immediate cause of death.' Again, his voice was flat. 'She also had pneumonia, as well as other infections—yeast and bacterial infections—that were proving impossible to treat.'

She nodded in commiseration. 'I'm so sorry, Blake,' she said, flushing as she realized that she had used his first name. It somehow added a touch of intimacy to their encounter which had been sorely lacking. 'Although it may not be much consolation to say so, it was a good way to die for someone who was already unconscious.'

'Yes…'

For a few minutes they sipped their drinks in silence. Abby was as taut as the proverbial bow.

'Thank you for the effort that you made, Abby,' he said. 'I'm afraid my behavior was rather churlish at the time. I do appreciate what you did.'

'Do you…do you want to talk about it, Blake?' she said softly. 'I can keep a confidence, I don't gossip. Stewart Hadley told me something of the circumstances. I didn't read the case history, actually. It seemed too private somehow.'

'Kaitlin and I,' he began hesitantly, as though talking about himself was difficult, 'had not lived as husband and wife for some time—several years—although we occupied the same house and continued to be united parents to our children. Neither of us believe—believed—in divorce while there are young children to take care of. We married young…too young. She was only twenty, I was twenty-five. It was a stupid thing to do, but we were headstrong in the way of youth—we thought we knew best.'

For a while he continued to talk, filling her in on his background.

'What went wrong?' Abby asked, sensing that he wanted to tell her that but was having difficulty broaching it.

'I wasn't a good husband to Kaitlin,' he confessed, his

voice barely audible. 'I failed to see, until it was too late, that she needed more than a lovely home with all the material things and a couple of kids. At first she seemed to thrive on it; she was like a little girl playing house. Then she grew up.'

'Go on,' Abby said.

'Apart from all that material stuff, all I gave her was the chance to wait home alone almost every evening, waiting for me to come home, while I did my thing at the hospital...the great man, saving lives.' There was self-loathing in his voice.

'You did save lives, Blake,' Abby said, keeping her voice matter-of-fact, although she felt like weeping and she longed to reach forward to touch his hands which he held clenched in front of him as he leaned forward to talk to her.

'Yes, now and then I did,' he agreed bitterly. 'But at what cost? The consequences were that a young woman was forced to look for love, for companionship, outside her marriage. She told me, more than once, that one of the reasons you marry someone is to spend a certain minimum amount of time with them. I ignored that need.'

'Didn't you love her?' Abby ventured, a need to know overwhelming her natural reticence.

'Of course I loved her. But I was hardly ever *there*. She was lonely. She needed affection and attention, two things that I didn't give her, except sporadically when I deigned to do so and it fitted in with work. I guess I took her for granted.' He looked at Abby with unseeing eyes, then looked across the room, as though he could see into the painful past.

'It's a common story, I'm afraid,' she said quietly. 'Doctors tend to think that the job they're doing is the most important one in the world... We're all guilty of it. What we have to realize is that a child only has one real daddy, one real mummy…and that a husband or wife needs time too.'

'Mmm… Why do we do it, Abby? Why do we do it?' He put his head in his hands for a moment, running his fingers down over his closed eyes, as though he could wipe away the images that tormented him.

'There's so much that's arbitrary about life,' she said. 'I think one of the reasons some of us work so compulsively is to try to impose some order on that arbitrariness…that chaos.'

'Mmm…'

'I can't really talk, can I?' she said, with a rueful little smile, feeling that she wished he would cry so that she could cry with him. 'I haven't got a husband or children.'

'Now I can see that all marriage did for Kaitlin was remove her from the sphere of other men, tantamount to putting her into purdah,' he said. 'Then, eventually, she looked outside marriage for the attention that I didn't give her.'

'Circumstances had a lot to do with it,' Abby said. 'We all know that medicine is a very demanding job, that it doesn't leave much time or energy. We all get drawn into it, Blake.' Even as she uttered the comforting words, true enough in themselves, she acknowledged that a lot of her sympathy was with the young Kaitlin, as well as with Blake himself.

'Mmm,' he said broodingly. 'We kid ourselves that we can have it all…then we ruin someone else's life by sucking them into our own myth. We prove inadequate to their needs.'

'Stop it, Blake!' Abby said, at last reaching forward to touch his hand briefly. 'There's no point in blaming yourself entirely.'

'I *do* blame myself. Kaitlin was too young to protest much at first, too inexperienced with men. And for a while she, too, was taken in by the myth that the most important part of my life was elsewhere.'

'Where does Todd Braxton come in?'

'He was the last of several boyfriends,' he said. 'Eventually she discovered that other men would love her...would give her what she needed. She was a sweet kid, beautiful, very loving. She needed fun, like all young people. That was something else I didn't give her. In many ways, I destroyed her.'

'Oh, Blake,' Abby breathed the words. What could one possibly say to that self-accusation? It at least held some truth. 'We all let other people down in some way, even when we are trying not to. We cannot be all things to them.'

'Maybe not. I could have been more to her, Abby, that's all. As long as I live, I shall not forgive myself.'

The bitterness in his tone was heartbreaking. She did not think for a minute that he was going through the motions of regret. Everything about him so far had indicated that his conscience was deep and far-reaching.

At last he leaned back against the cushions of the sofa, letting out his breath on a sigh. Absently he cupped the mug of chocolate with both hands.

'Your drink will be cold soon,' she prompted.

This time the silence was less tense. There was a certain sympathy between them so she, too, was able to relax in the chair she had drawn up near him. Thoughtfully she sipped her drink. There was little she could say really— better just to listen. Just to be there with him was something in itself.

'So many of the tragedies of life are prosaic, mundane in their origins...not heroic. What happened to Kaitlin would be almost slapstick if the outcome had not been so unbelievably awful,' he said, his voice husky with grief, as though he were thinking aloud.

'How...how was it discovered that she was HIV positive?' Abby asked.

'They did the test in Jamaica after the accident. It was done again when she was brought back here in case it was a false positive.'

'I see,' Abby said.

'I had myself checked out…to see if I had maybe given it to her four years ago. That would just about have finished me off.'

'Four years ago?'

'That was about the last time we were together as husband and wife.'

'Oh…'

It was perhaps fortuitous that the telephone rang a moment later, the sound cutting sharply into the silence as they paused. To Abby, the interruption came as a relief. She wanted to be alone to cry, a nameless regret of her own adding to his abject guilt. There was nothing maudlin about Blake—he accepted his guilt as a matter of course.

'This is the locating service at University Hospital,' the voice said when she answered the telephone. 'There's a message for you, Dr Gibson, from a patient, Kyra Trenton. She says could you please call her before the weekend is over? It's very important, but not urgent. Here's the number…'

For a few seconds Abby's mind was blank. 'Kyra Trenton?' She murmured the name. 'Ah, yes.' Then she remembered the pregnant sixteen-year-old girl. Hastily she scribbled the number on a pad, aware that Blake had stood up.

'I must go, Abby,' he said, looking restless, with his hands in the pockets of his trousers, as though he wished to hide the tension in them. 'I've taken up too much of your time.'

'No you haven't,' she contradicted him. 'You don't have to go yet…'

'Don't I?' He managed a brief smile. 'I don't want to be

too much of a pain in the ass. You've been very understanding, very sweet.'

For a few moments they stood looking at each other,
standing close. 'I think you would do the same for me,
Blake, if I were in the same sort of trouble,' she said truthfully, looking him full in the face, engaging his tortured
eyes with her own frank regard, 'in spite of what you've
told me about neglecting your wife.'

Without knowing quite how it happened, they reached
for each other at the same moment and were all of a sudden
in each other's arms. Abby felt his strong arms crushing
her to him, her face pressed sideways against his broad
chest. She closed her eyes in abject relief. It was going to
be all right; he did not blame her for anything. Her arms
were around his waist, returning the comforting pressure.

There was nothing sexual in their embrace—it was a hug
of need, conferring comfort. Abby found that she wanted
to stay there, in the circle of his arms; she allowed herself
to relax forward against him.

'Thank you, Abby, for listening,' he said softly, 'You're
going to make a fine GP...one of the best.'

'Thank you,' she said, her voice breaking.

He was stroking her hair, leaning his face against the top
of her head. They drew a strange kind of comfort from each
other, while the mood was one of mourning.

There was a long way to go if she were ever to get close
to Blake in any other sense. Desperately, as she seemed to
be standing on one side of a huge void, she wanted that
closeness, even though he had as good as said that he
wasn't capable of giving it. She didn't believe it. She felt
a strange sense of destiny...an intimation of something that
she had felt when she had first met him.

'You're very sweet, Abby,' he said again. He kissed the
top of her head absently, as one might kiss a child in a
moment of high emotion.

'Maybe I am sweet, Blake. I'm also tough. I've had to be.'

'From now on, I shall try to think of you as both, then.' There was tenderness in his voice, it seemed to her. 'Thank you, anyway.'

They stood together for a long moment, some of the tension draining away, then he drew away from her.

'I have to go now...my children will be wondering where I am,' he said. 'They're very vulnerable right now, of course.'

When he released her it was all she could do not to grasp his hands to make him stay. 'Well, goodnight, Blake,' she said. 'I'm here most evenings, if you feel the need to talk.'

'I'll remember that. I'll see myself out.' At the door he turned to her. 'The garden party has been cancelled for Saturday, of course. It's been put off for two weeks. I couldn't cancel it completely—the caterers plan this thing for a long time in advance. It's an annual event.'

'I see.'

'I'm going to take a few days off, but I don't want to leave Mr Simmons for too long. I like to be around myself. I'll see you some time next week. Goodbye.'

'Yes. Goodbye.'

As Abby closed her door she acknowledged that he had, by his last remarks, summed up the dilemma for the doctor who had seriously ill patients relying on his continual presence.

CHAPTER EIGHT

'MY MOTHER'S in Gresham. She turned up unexpectedly,' Kyra Trenton told Abby when she telephoned her fifteen minutes later, even though it was late, having dragged her concentration away from Blake back to work mode and the message she had received from the locating service.

'Go on,' Abby encouraged.

'Thank you for talking to me…for letting me call you at home. This is my mother's apartment I'm calling from,' the girl said in a low voice. 'She's sleeping right now. I…I've sort of come round to the idea that maybe I should tell her that I'm pregnant. I want to…to ask your advice, Dr Gibson. And I was wondering whether, maybe, you would tell her…' the voice trailed off.

'So you haven't actually made up your mind whether you want her to know, Kyra?' Abby spoke gently, not fooled by the note of bravado in the girl's voice. She knew it was a façade that had been built up to hide extreme vulnerability, a façade that could crumble very easily.

'No.'

'Well, Kyra,' Abby said, trying to sort out her thoughts quickly, striving to give the girl good advice, 'since I don't know your mother, you will have to give me some idea of whether she would be supportive of you…of how you think she would react at the news. You will have to judge by how she has reacted in the past to serious news…a crisis.'

There was a silence at the other end, during which Abby could almost see the girl frowning, biting her lip in concentration. It must have taken considerable courage on her part to have contacted the hospital to get in touch with her.

'I'm…not sure. She's pretty good, I think. She's a very

put-together sort of woman. But I don't know whether she would rather not know…then she wouldn't have to deal with it, would she? And I would die if she told my father, if this got out in any way.'

How sad it was that this girl did not feel she knew her mother well enough to know how she would react…or so it seemed. 'Do you think she would be likely to tell your father?' Abby said gently. 'Would she tell him if you asked her not to? And would she support your decision about the abortion?'

Again there was a silence.

'I'll certainly talk to her if you want me to, Kyra,' Abby said. 'I assume that she's going back to Ottawa on Monday so you'd like me to talk to her at the weekend—if we agree that she should be told?'

'Yes.'

'Look, Kyra, I think you need to consider this a little longer. I'm going to be home now for the rest of the evening so why don't you mull it over some more, then call me back when you've decided? At the latest, call me tomorrow morning at about a quarter to eight. Can you do that? You'll have the night to sleep on it, then.'

'Sure.'

'I'll go along with whatever you want. Think about how you're going to feel in the long term if she doesn't know…and, conversely, if she does know. Try to imagine what the outcome would be in each scenario, and whether you will one day want to tell her if you don't tell her now… And how she would feel because you *hadn't* told her before the event. '

'Yes. Thank you, Dr Gibson.'

This is really what general practice is going to be like, considered Abby pensively as she changed back moments later into her dressing-gown. It meant getting more immersed in her patients' personal lives, rather than doing the dramatic resuscitation thing she had done with Kaitlin

Contini. There would be times, she knew, when she would miss the drama and immediacy of the other. Yet this was what she felt she was good at, what she wanted to do—try to help people in the broad aspects of their lives.

'A cup of tea is in order, I think,' she said aloud. 'A little relaxation, a little TLC for the self.'

Kyra called back at precisely a quarter to eight the next morning, just as Abby was ready to leave for work, making her hope that Kyra had not been sitting for hours by the telephone, waiting to call.

'Dr Gibson, I've decided that she should know,' the girl's tentative voice informed her. 'I don't know how we should go about it. You see, I...I would rather not be around when you tell her...if you don't mind...I want to give her a chance to cool off. There's no way I could get her to come with me to the clinic at the hospital...without telling her first why I wanted her to go there.'

'Perhaps I should come to your apartment, let you slip out, then tell her, Kyra.'

'You...you wouldn't mind?'

'No. One of the first things she may want to know, Kyra, is the name of the boy responsible. I assume you've considered that. It's a natural reaction, I'm afraid.'

'That's one thing I don't want her to know! Must she?'

'No. She may be persistent, though.'

'I don't want her to try to get any sort of revenge on him. He's a sweet guy. He didn't do it on purpose, and...like I said before...he doesn't know I'm pregnant. It would really destroy him if he knew.'

Abby kept her mouth shut on that one, believing that the less said at this point, the better. 'What would be a good time, then?'

'Um...Sunday? A bit before eleven o'clock?'

'Sure, that's fine. Now, you call me if there's any change. Ok?'

'I've just thought of the perfect excuse to be out,' Kyra added, sounding more hopeful. 'I'll go to church. I know she won't want to come because she's got stuff to do at the apartment—sorting out her summer clothes, stuff like that.'

'I'll be there, Kyra. Bye for now… And try not to worry. We'll sort it all out.'

It seemed odd to be at work later, knowing that Blake would not be anywhere in the various multi-story buildings that made up the huge edifice of University Hospital. As she walked the corridors, answered the telephone, went to see patients on the floors, attended Outpatient clinics, a sense of longing never left her. There was also the sobering awareness that, in spite of her strivings to the contrary, she had definitely become emotionally involved with the new head of the internal medicine department.

Sunday dawned bright, but the weather forecast that Abby listened to on the radio as she ate her breakfast predicted showers in the afternoon. She planned to take a bus and then walk part of the way to the apartment that belonged to the Trenton family. It was in a wealthy residential area near downtown, not far from where Blake lived.

As she left her own place, she considered how nearly unprecedented it was for a GP in this day and age, in this place, to make a home visit of any sort. There was a lot to be said for it, even though it was time-consuming. She felt the girl needed it.

The apartment building was only two storeys high, blending in with the imposing, beautiful houses with which it shared the street. There were big trees and lawns, a greenness that belied its position in the centre of a city. Kyra, wearing a neat coat, was waiting for her at the main entrance.

'I'm so glad you've come, Dr Gibson,' she addressed Abby in a breathless rush. 'My mother thinks I'm on my

way to church right now, but I'll have to take you up and
introduce you to her quickly. I'm sorry to do it this way…I
couldn't think of anything else.'

Kyra looked absurdly young, about thirteen, with her
pale hair pulled back in a short ponytail, her face devoid
of any sort of make-up.

'Don't worry, Kyra,' Abby said, 'I'll deal with it.'

They went up in an elevator to the second floor. Abby
had dressed carefully for the occasion, with a skirt and
blouse under a lightweight coat and her best leather handbag and matching shoes. As the wife of a member of parliament, Mrs Trenton would be a sophisticated woman.

With rather clumsy fingers, Kyra opened the door of the
apartment. Abby followed her into a spacious hallway, then
into a sitting room.

'Mummy!' Kyra called, 'Can you come here for a minute?'

A tall, slim, middle-aged woman, dressed in a floral silk
robe and bedroom slippers, came in. She had pale blonde
hair, smoothly cut in a classic bob, that framed her lean
face. She still had a light tan from a winter holiday obviously spent in a tropical climate, making Abby think of the
bleakness of winter in Gresham and her own pale skin.

'I thought you were going to church, dear.' Mrs Trenton
frowned at her daughter, then looked questioningly at
Abby, too polite to ask her who she was, waiting to be
introduced.

'I am going. This is a friend of mine, Mummy.
She…um…she would like to talk to you about something.'
With that, the girl looked frantically at Abby.

With a nod and smile to indicate that Kyra could leave,
Abby took over. 'I probably won't be here when you get
back, Kyra. I'll see you later this week.'

Quickly the girl left.

'I'm sorry to barge in on you like this, Mrs Trenton. I'm

Dr Gibson, your daughter's GP. She asked me to talk to you.'

'What is all this about?' Mrs Trenton looked bewildered. 'Is Kyra sick? She said absolutely nothing about this to me.'

'Perhaps we could sit down.' They were in a very large, comfortable sitting room off the hallway.

'Well…yes, of course. Come in. Please, take your coat off.'

In the sitting room Mrs Trenton sat on a wing chair, the expression on her face apprehensive yet polite, while Abby took off her coat and sat opposite her.

'No, Kyra isn't sick, Mrs Trenton. I'm afraid she's pregnant…about six weeks pregnant.'

Mrs. Trenton's mouth dropped open slightly, her eyes widened and she put her hand up to her mouth. 'Oh, my God!' she said.

'At first she didn't want to tell you,' Abby went on levelly. 'She changed her mind because you came unexpectedly. She's decided to have an abortion. She's under the care of a gynecologist at University Hospital. In fact, she's booked to be admitted to the day surgery unit this coming week.'

'Oh, my God!' the woman repeated, staring at Abby. 'Are you sure? I mean…is it absolutely certain?'

'Yes. We did a pregnancy test, as Kyra did herself. There's no doubt.'

The woman lay back in the chair and closed her eyes, letting out her breath on a long sigh then not speaking for quite a while.

'We—my husband and I,' she said wearily at last, 'only agreed to let her stay here in this city because she would be a weekly boarder at her school. She insisted on staying at that school, instead of moving with us. I didn't dream that something like this would happen. Who else knows about this?'

'No one. She didn't want you or her father to know at first. She's living in fear that it will get out...into the newspapers.'

Again Mrs Trenton closed her eyes. 'Poor darling,' she said, her voice agonized. 'To think that she had to be alone. I'll stay here, of course, to be with her. I...I guess I've neglected her in recent months, ever since we moved to Ottawa. One tends to think one's children are more sophisticated than they actually are.'

'Yes.'

'Did she tell you who was responsible, who got her pregnant?'

'No. She doesn't want to divulge that information.'

'It wasn't...?'

'No, it wasn't rape,' Abby said gently. 'I think it was one of those innocent things, probably after a school dance or something...an accident. Apparently the boy doesn't know she's pregnant.'

'Oh, dear. Well, we shall just have to deal with it the best we can. I'm not going to be angry. I hope she didn't think...' The woman's voice trailed off and she bit her lip, as though fighting tears.

The door of the apartment slammed. Both women turned their heads as Kyra came into the room. 'I couldn't go to church,' the girl blurted out. 'I've just been walking around outside.'

Mrs Trenton got up and held out her arms. 'You could have told me, dear,' she said gently. 'You could have told me right away.'

'I was frightened.' Kyra ran forward into her mother's arms. In a moment she was sobbing, her face muffled against her mother's chest, while Mrs Trenton enclosed her tightly in her arms.

'Of course you were,' she soothed. 'You don't have to think that I wouldn't be there for you. I know it may not seem like it at times, but I've always put you first—you and your brother and sister—before your father, before my-self certainly. I will always be there.'

They were both crying quietly now. Abby could see the relief in Kyra at the letting-go. Unobtrusively she put on her coat, her work done for now.

'I'll stay in Gresham now—make some excuse for being here. It's all right, baby.'

'Thank you, Dr Gibson,' Kyra said tearfully, as she saw Abby preparing to leave. 'Thank you so much.'

'Will you be all right now?' Abby said.

'Yes.'

'Will you call me later this evening so that I know that your plans have not changed?'

The girl nodded, managing a smile. The change in her was dramatic, just knowing that her mother was on her side.

'I'll find my own way out,' Abby said softly.

On the Wednesday of that week she saw Blake again for the first time since his visit to her apartment. There he was, in the office of the second-floor unit where Mr Simmons had his room.

'Oh, good morning,' she said hesitantly, as she hurried into the office to look up the latest treatment on their patient, which would be on the computer. Nurses were going in and out busily.

It was good to see Blake, yet his wife's death had some-how formed a barrier between them in spite of his talk with her afterwards. There was a distancing so that she could not bring herself to use his first name in this work setting. 'How are you?' she added instead.

'Good morning, Abby. I'm all right.' His face was un-smiling, strained. 'I was about to see Mr Simmons. I as-sume that's why you're here?'

'Yes. I thought I would see him now that his first in-duction chemotherapy has come to an end. He's probably still feeling pretty low.'

'Yes. He'll stay in hospital for another three weeks or so, then he'll be at home for another four to six weeks, then we'll get him in again for the first consolidation chemo.'

Abby nodded. After that there would be a second consolidation treatment, then possibly a bone marrow transplant, if necessary.

'We may as well go in together,' Blake said.

Mr Simmons was propped up in bed when they entered in their anti-infection garb. He looked ill, pale and gaunt, older than his sixty-three years. Abby was glad of the enveloping headgear, the face mask, to hide her sense of shock as she looked at him. Several times before she had seen patients after chemotherapy, but she did not remember seeing anyone look as exhausted as Ralph Simmons.

'Hello, Mr Simmons.' She was the first to speak, going up quietly to the bed to touch his hand. 'This is Dr Gibson. Dr Contini and I have come to see you. How are you feeling?'

Peering at them through half-closed lids, as though he did not want to let in too much light, he groaned slightly.

'Trying to convince myself that I'm feeling better than I did when I woke up... Not succeeding very well, I'm afraid. I'm glad to be here...' His voice was husky, barely audible.

Abby stood silently, going through the information on the bedside computer, while Blake talked to their patient about the treatment he would be receiving before he was discharged.

When they were ready to leave, Abby touched their patient's hand again.

'Hang in there, Mr Simmons,' she said. 'You really will feel better in a day or two.'

Before she turned to go he grasped her hand. '"To every thing there is a season,"' he quoted, his voice painfully slow and laboured, '"and a time to every purpose under the heaven..."'

Abby was conscious of Blake standing very still beside her and she could not look at him as the image of Kaitlin came to her mind. She had no doubt that he was thinking of her too.

'''A time to be born and a time to die...''' The voice became quieter, slurring the words. '''A time to break down and a time to build up, a time to weep and a time to laugh...a time to get and a time to lose; a time to keep and a time to cast away... A time to love...''' His voice stopped and he appeared to sleep.

Moving awkwardly in the enveloping gown that came down to her feet, Abby left the room ahead of Blake and went to the women's change room to remove the protective clothing. There were tears in her eyes, which she blinked rapidly away. 'A time to love'. The words echoed in her mind. Was it her imagination, or did she sense that Blake was thinking about that too?

Out in the corridor she almost collided with a woman who was hovering near the door. At first she did not recognize her, then saw that it was the woman in the photograph that Ralph Simmons had displayed on his bedside table before his chemo had begun, a face that looked decidedly more worn than the fresh young face in the picture.

'Are you Dr Gibson?'

'Yes, I am. You must be Mrs Simmons.'

'Yes... He told me about you, Dr Gibson. You've helped him a lot by just talking to him,' the young woman said. 'Thank you for doing that.'

Blake came out then. 'Hi, Mrs Simmons,' he said. 'Your husband's doing great. The way he looks now is normal for this stage so don't be alarmed.'

For some time Blake talked to her, kindly, never talking down to her. Abby wondered how he could do it when he must be suffering so much himself. Maybe that was how he found comfort. At the same time, she knew intuitively that if she had to do it herself under the same circumstances she would rise to the occasion. After all, it was part of the job. She prayed that she would not be so tested for a very long time.

'I'm going in to see him now,' Mrs Simmons said. The expression on her face had smoothed out. 'Thank you.'

Blake put a commiserating hand on her arm. 'He's a fighter, that husband of yours,' he assured her with a smile. 'I expect you know that. After all, he's got a lot to live for.'

The relieved smile on the woman's face encompassed both doctors as she turned to go to the change room. 'Yes,' she said.

'Got time for a quick coffee in the cafeteria, Abby?' Blake said.

'Well…' Abby looked at her watch, knowing that she would say yes, whatever the time, even though there was still a niggling fear in her that he might not completely trust her after the intubation of his wife. 'I could certainly use a coffee, and since it's practically right next door to the clinic I have to go to, yes.'

'Good. I'll treat you.' They set off at a brisk pace along the busy corridor.

'You don't have to,' she said, smiling, feeling her spirits lift.

'Every fifty cents helps when you're a struggling GP.' He smiled back, the action lightening his features. Perhaps things were going to be all right after all between them.

The words that Mr Simmons had quoted repeated themselves in her brain… 'a time to love'… 'a time to love'. Was this her time to love? And was it to be this man?

Sitting in the huge cafeteria on the main floor of the hospital, a place that always buzzed with conversation and activity, with two mugs of steaming coffee in front of them, Abby found herself blurting out the story of Kyra Trenton and how she had gone to talk to the girl's mother.

'She's been on my mind so much,' she finished up. 'I've

tried to advise her as best I can…but I don't know whether
I'm doing the right things. My instinct is that she should
have the abortion, continue in school, go to university. But
what if she regrets it in a few years' time?'

'That's a risk you have to take,' Blake said, looking at
her levelly. 'All that you and the girl can do is what you
both feel to be right *now*—not try to second-guess what
will seem right one or two years from now. If you do that
too often you become habitually indecisive and never make
a definite decision about anything. Not that you don't have
to think it through carefully, of course, but once you've
made the decision, accept it. You win some and you lose
some.'

'Mmm…' She nodded.

'All you can really do is listen to the girl and tell her
what is available, then the decision will have to be hers.
From what I know of young people of her age, they often
instinctively make the decision that is right for them in
something like this, at the stage of life they're at, when it
comes to the crunch. A little fear sobers them up. She'll be
fine, so long as she's got someone on her side.'

'You sound very wise,' she commented, a little shyly.

'Not always wise for myself, Abby,' he said quietly. 'But
I've got two sons, remember?' Again he smiled, that slow,
warm smile, in spite of his underlying strain. That smile
did very positive things to her. 'It's often easier to sort out
other people's problems, isn't it? I'm sure glad at this moment that I haven't got a sixteen-year-old daughter.'

Abby found herself smiling back, her eyes held by his.
'How are your sons?' she said.

'They took the news as though they were not surprised.
Maybe they have more perspicacity than I had given them
credit for,' he said thoughtfully, his face reverting to something of its original tiredness. 'They were—are—very upset, of course. They need time to mourn.'

'And you?'

'Yes, I need to mourn,' he said slowly. 'It's somewhat different for me. I let go of Kaitlin emotionally quite a long time ago. She let go first. What I have to deal with is something different—not being much good as a husband, as a companion. Like many people, I wish I could put the clock back...'

She wanted to ask him what he would do differently if he could do just that, but she did not have the nerve to put her thoughts into words. Would he strive to be more accessible to Kaitlin? Or would he not have married her? The questions remained unasked.

'How is Will Ryles?' she asked.

'Healthwise he's doing well. We, his friends, seem to be making some headway in saving the integrity of his department, too.'

'Permanently?'

'We hope so. He should be able to go home in a day or two. He'll come up to the cardiac clinic as an outpatient.'

'I'm so glad he's all right so far. Well, I—I have to get to the outpatient clinic now,' she said, catching sight of a wall clock. 'Thank you for the coffee.'

He nodded. 'I hope to see you at my garden party. Since it can't be put off permanently—too many arrangements have been made—we might as well make the best of it. I'll need some young, smiling faces there,' he said.

'I can't absolutely guarantee that mine will be smiling,' she said, standing up, 'but I'll do my best. Yes, I hope to be there.'

As she walked out of the cafeteria, she dragged her thoughts with difficulty away from Blake Contini. Later that day she was to meet Kyra Trenton and her mother, to have a final talk before the girl came into the day surgery unit later that week for her operation. It was all arranged, but there was still time for the girl to back out if she wanted to. Mrs Trenton also wanted to meet the gynecologist. Time was of the essence now.

Her thoughts turned from the young girl to the middle-aged Gary Barlow, whose radiology report had come back with a diagnosis of probable lung cancer. Fortunately, it was only in one lobe of the right lung. They had booked him for another test in the X-ray department, computerized axial tomography—CAT scan for short—which would give a much more detailed picture of the tumor.

After that, he would have to be referred to a chest surgeon and come into hospital for an examination of his lungs with a bronchoscope, and for a needle biopsy of the lung at the same time. These would be done in the operating rooms under a general anesthetic.

Abby geared herself up mentally as she entered the familiar outpatient clinic rooms. One good thing—it had been Dr Wharton, not her, who had had to break the news to Mr Barlow that he had probable lung cancer, giving him also the good news that it appeared to be confined to one area. Mr Barlow had stopped smoking instantly, apparently, but, of course, it was too late.

If the pathology report came back, from the biopsies, confirming that he had cancer, then he would have to have the lobe of his lung removed and hope that it had not already spread to other parts of his body...

CHAPTER NINE

THE day for the garden party dawned warm and clear, a beautiful summer day of chirping birds and burgeoning nature that promised to be hot in the afternoon, with possible thunder later.

Arriving by taxi in the afternoon at the Contini residence, to find a big house surrounded by lawns and extensive gardens, Abby felt suddenly shy, realizing that she really knew little about Blake. As the taxi drew away, leaving her standing alone at massive wrought-iron gates which had been flung wide to receive guests, she wondered whether she would feel like the proverbial fish out of water.

A huge tent had been erected on a lawn at the side of the house, where formal waiters moved busily to and fro among long tables. So this was clearly not going to be a simple barbecue, as Blake had implied—it was to be something much more formal. Already a small crowd of guests was milling around a drinks table, the sounds of laughter and chatter spilling out to the quiet residential road which was not far from the centre of Gresham.

Two cars drew up and disgorged more guests. Making her way through the gate and moving in behind these new arrivals, Abby had the feeling that she was going to be one of the youngest of the guests, if the other guests so far were anything to go by. They were mostly middle-aged and older, as far as she could see, the upper crust of the hospital administration and the medical profession.

Almost wishing that she could retreat, she felt nervous until Blake came towards the group to which she had attached herself. She waited until he had greeted them, and she was the only one left.

'Abby,' he said, coming up to her. 'Nice to see you.'

His eyes went over her, taking in the delicate, close-fitting, floral crêpe dress, calf-length, that she wore, which wrapped itself close to her body as a breeze blew through the garden. She wondered what he would say if he knew that she had bought the dress at a vintage clothing store for fifteen dollars, a place where she bought most of her clothes. Over one arm she carried a gossamer-thin wool jacket. She had left her hair loose, its shiny, wavy strands subdued under a simple straw hat.

There had been a lot of kissing among the guests, usually on both cheeks, which Abby always found slightly affected when indulged in by people who didn't know each other well personally, or among those who did not really like each other—which was often the case among these hospital types in the days of budget cuts. Yet with Blake, in those few seconds when he held out a welcoming hand to her, Abby found herself holding her breath, waiting for him to kiss her.

The warmth of his hand enveloped hers. As he leaned towards her, she turned her cheek automatically. Then his face was against hers, his lips brushing her skin. The contact seemed to take place in a timeless moment in which she was conscious only of his touch.

When he drew back slowly, their eyes met. 'Did you drive?' he said prosaically.

'No, I came by taxi. I don't own a car.'

'Then perhaps I can drive you home,' he offered, 'especially if you stay to the end. There's going to be dancing a little later on, for which I've found a good band.' He took her elbow, chatting to put her at ease. 'Come, I'll introduce you to the bartender—get you a drink—and to the only other medical resident to arrive so far.'

The other resident proved to be Tim Barrick, who seemed just as relieved to see her as she was to see him. 'You know each other, I think.' Blake smiled at them, guessing their reservations. 'Get yourselves drinks, have a good time.'

As more guests arrived, Blake left Tim and Abby to their own devices, with a murmured, 'Talk to you later.'

Although pale and tired-looking, only those who knew him well could probably have told that he was suffering from the loss of his wife. There was an added air of distraction about him which had not been there when Abby had first met him, she decided as she thoughtfully watched him walk away from her.

'He led me to believe this was a simple nosh-up under a tree, with hamburgers on a smoky barbecue pit,' Tim said to her when Blake was out of earshot. 'Not some raving royal garden party.'

The expression on his face was so pained that Abby threw back her head and laughed delightedly. Taking Tim's arm, she drew him towards the food tent. 'Maybe he knew we wouldn't come otherwise. Let's get some food, Tim, I'm starving. We're going to enjoy ourselves, see how the wealthy live. OK?'

At the same time, she felt an odd sense of something like mourning. The vague hopes she had harboured about Blake Contini receded further and further into a world of fantasy where, apparently, they belonged.

It seemed to her that not only was Blake Contini still emotionally involved with his former wife, in spite of his denials, and the father of two sons, it was probable that he would not be interested in a young woman like herself who had to buy her clothes from a thrift shop in order to pay off student loans.

For the past few nights she had not slept well. She had tossed and turned, thinking about Kaitlin. Had she found being a doctor's wife very difficult? Had that been why she had found it necessary to have a lover when her husband seemed to be everything that a woman would want?

'Hang on,' Tim said, breaking into her thoughts. 'Get

yourself a couple of glasses of wine first, then you won't give a damn who's watching you. We're going to need that—there's that odious Ronald Slater, the big guy, just coming through the gate.'

A little later, with glasses of wine in hand, they made their way to the food tent. Abby glanced over her shoulder to see Blake talking to the CEO of University Hospital. 'I didn't think Ronald Slater would be here,' she commented thoughtfully. 'I had got the impression that Dr Contini didn't like him.'

'That may be so,' Tim said, 'but you have to live with these people, so liking doesn't come into it. I guess the whole odious bunch will be here. You have to play your cards right in that hospital, otherwise you could be out pronto.'

'Hmm,' Abby said pensively, her eyes going over the array of delicious food before them, her mind on Will Ryles and the conspiracies he was convinced were being hatched to run down his department to the point where it might self-destruct.

'Come on, Abby,' Tim urged, helping himself to a gen-erous portion of smoked salmon topped with pickled ca-pers. 'Eat, drink and be merry, for tomorrow we're on call.'

'You're right, Tim.' Abby smiled. 'To compensate, I'll have some of those giant prawns and some of that aspar-agus in aspic, just to start.'

'Attagirl! Don't forget to take a good slug of that wine in between mouthfuls.'

By the time the music started later, the high volume of conversation and laughter was hardly drowned out by it.

Abby and Tim had drunk a fair amount of wine at that point. The amplifiers were needed to override conversation in the big tent, and get people to take to the polished wooden dance floor that had been set up at one end. This was not going to be a function that went on late into the evening, but clearly Blake had planned to make the event fun for those who stayed for more than an hour or so.

Abby was feeling decidedly dizzy from wine and lack of sleep when Tim leaned against her and slurred the words, 'Care to dansh?'

'Love to...' Abby giggled, propping him up '...provided that you promise to drink several cups of strong coffee before driving home.' They moved out onto the small dance floor.

'Not driving,' Tim said. 'Walking.'

'Even so,' she said, as they supported each other, swaying back and forth in time to the music. For some time now she had noted that Blake was dancing, going from one unattached woman to another, no doubt making them feel welcome. Admitting to twinges of envy as she surreptitiously watched him and propped up Tim at the same time, she longed for him to come to her.

'Got to go to the bathroom,' Tim said after a spate of particularly vigorous movement. 'Get a glass of water.'

'Are you all right?'

'Yesh...'

'Not going to throw up, are you, Tim? If you are, I shall maybe have to pretend I'm not with you.'

'Nope. Everyone knows you're with me, Abby.'

Abby picked her way to the edge of the dance floor as Tim weaved his way out of the throng towards the house. Unexpectedly, her arm was grasped and she was eased round to face her host.

'Not going, I hope, before I've had a dance?' Blake said, looking down at her quizzically. 'Are you enjoying it?'

'Yes...very much,' She said truthfully as she stumbled slightly against him so that he moved to steady her, making her acutely aware of his tall, taut and muscular body, elegantly casual in an open-necked shirt and light pants. At that moment, as he held her, he seemed oddly dear and familiar to her in that crowd, yet at the same time sophisticated and remote from her world.

'I'm feeling a little dizzy—too much wine, not enough sleep, I think,' she explained. 'Not drunk, though.' She looked up at him as his arms tightened around her. 'Can still dance.'

'Good.' There was a suggestion that he was laughing at her, or maybe with her.

In his arms she leaned against him stiffly, yet allowed herself to enjoy the close contact. He took her hands and placed them around his neck. 'Hang on to me,' he murmured.

'I'm not drunk,' she said indignantly, her fingers inadvertently touching the warm skin of his neck above the collar of his shirt.

'No, of course not.' He gave a slow grin that lightened his handsome face so that Abby found herself smiling back, captivated by him, pleased that she could make him smile.

She remembered the pale bleakness of his features after the death of his wife. Try as she may, she could not get that image out of her mind. Perversely, words he had uttered also came back to her: 'I let go of Kaitlin emotionally quite a long time ago.'

'Is this a duty dance?' she enquired, tilting back her head to look up at him.

'No, Abby,' He looked down at her, his face close to hers. 'I left you till last. This is pure pleasure.'

He gathered her against him on the crowded dance floor where there was scarcely room to move and no one could wonder why they were so close. In moments her whole body was tingling with a rare ecstasy, a feeling that she belonged there in his arms. Much as she told herself that it was madness to feel that, it was nonetheless, a fact.

If he was affected by her in the same way, he did not show it openly, yet she sensed an inner stillness, as though he were aware only of her in the entire place, that he was

not indifferent to her or just dancing with her out of politeness. Chiding herself, telling herself not to presume, she
gave herself up to the moment. If only she had been more
experienced with men in this way, she would have engaged
in sophisticated repartee, disguising her emotions. As it
was, she was speechless.

More and more couples crammed, laughing, into the tiny
space. Dimly she spotted Tim on the outskirts, searching
the crowd for her. Some of the other residents were with
him.

'I think there's going to be a downpour of rain,' Blake
said in her ear. Indeed, the beautiful blue sky had clouded
over earlier and a premature dusk had descended, bringing
with it a chill.

'Mmm,' she agreed, as his encircling arms tightened
slightly on her slim waist, pulling her against him. His lips
remained close to her ear and she could feel his warm
breath caressing the lobe.

People began to leave, with hasty goodbyes and apologies, about twenty minutes later as soon as the first large
drops of rain fell on the tarpaulin of the tent.

'Go into the house, Abby,' Blake invited, pulling away
from her to say goodbye to his departing guests. 'I'll drive
you home when the others have gone, if you'd like me to.'

'Thank you...yes.'

She hurried from the tent to the house, with the drops of
rain penetrating the thin crêpe of her dress. Soon there
would be a real downpour. In the sanctuary of the spacious
front hall she saw that several other people had taken shel-
ter there, among them Ronald Slater who stood squarely in
her way as she tried to veer around the throng to get to the
sweeping staircase and find a bathroom on the second floor.

'We haven't had the pleasure,' the CEO said, addressing
her, his eyes moving from her face to the outline of her
breasts and back again.

There was something suggestive in that look, the hint of

a proprietorial leer, that made Abby freeze. Without looking down at herself, she realized that the rain must have
made her dress semi-transparent in places, perhaps revealing the outline of her bra to his avid gaze. 'You're one of
the residents, I believe?' he said.

'Yes,' she said, unable to think of anything else to say
to him.

'How do you like University Hospital?' he said, his
small, shrewd eyes darting over her.

Recovering, Abby stared him full in the face. 'I'm in the
family practice program,' she said, unsmiling. 'It's fine, but
I can't wait to get out into the real world.'

By her tone she hoped she was letting him know that
she did not find the hothouse atmosphere of the hospital
these days to be representative of reality, or the deliberately
engineered crises which were largely excuses to take
money out of the already tight budget.

'Just as well,' he said, his pugilistic stance slightly threat-
ening. 'We've considered getting rid of the family practice
training program.'

'Oh, really?' she said, raising her eyebrows, not letting
him see her incipient apprehension. Having started into her
second year of training, it was unlikely that anything would
be axed that was in progress, anything that had a foresee-
able end anyway—or so she reassured herself. 'That would
be a mistake, surely?'

'Why?' he said bluntly.

'The hospital has such a good reputation for turning out
excellent GPs.'

'Huh,' he said, a cynical twist to his thick lips. 'Teaching
doesn't make money—it takes money.'

'But surely that is the mandate of a teaching hospital,'
Abby said sweetly. 'There are so many other places that
are in the business of making money, but not too many
providing excellent teaching.'

'Maybe' he said.

It was with a sense of relief that the small, tinny sound of the pager in her handbag punctuated the verbal impasse. 'Excuse me,' she said, heading for the stairs. Without looking back, she mounted the staircase, feeling that he was watching her—no doubt mentally undressing her as she went.

'Can I be of some assistance?' A female voice with an English accent addressed her from behind as she came to a halt on the spacious second-floor landing, having marched as quickly as possible away from that stare from below.

Turning, she was confronted by a youngish woman, a pretty woman with pale red hair and hazel eyes. Perhaps this was Blake's mistress. The thought came to Abby at once. Surely he would not be without a woman. The idea engendered a sharp stab of regret.

'I was looking for a bathroom,' Abby said, 'and a telephone, if possible. My pager just went off. I don't suppose it's anything important because I'm not on call, but I would like to answer it.'

'Of course.' The woman smiled. 'There's a bathroom for the ladies just around that corner…' she pointed '…and all the phones seem to be in use at the moment, but there are four lines coming into the house so you should get a free one soon. I'll show you where the guests' rooms are. I'm the nanny to the family.'

'Ah, I see.' Abby found herself smiling, an absurd sense of relief coming over her. Not that this attractive woman could not still be Blake's lover… At the moment she did not want to question her own feelings too closely.

The two guest-room telephones were in use so Abby decided to wait in the passage.

'There's a fourth line in Dr Contini's bedroom,' the nanny said. 'That room down there. I don't suppose he'll mind if you use it if these others go on too long.'

'Thanks.'

When she came out of the bathroom, the guest telephones were still in use so she paced up and down the passages, her feet sinking luxuriously into the thick pile of the carpet. As she hovered, two boys of about ten years of age came along the passage. She had not seen them outside at the barbecue. They were, she supposed, Blake's sons.

Expecting them to pass her, she was surprised that they stopped near her and looked at her with unsmiling faces, silently assessing her.

'Are you our father's girlfriend?' one of them said.

Maybe she was getting paranoid after her encounter with Ronald Slater, Abby speculated, but she detected hostility, a challenge, in the stance of both boys. Neither boy looked like Blake—or like their mother, come to that. They were more a mixture of both parents, with light brown hair and light blue eyes, even-featured.

'No, I'm not,' she said, meeting their speculative, un-smiling regard with a level look of her own, 'I'm a doctor at University Hospital, a colleague of his.'

The nanny was coming along the passage towards them. 'Mark! Jeremy!' she called. 'What are you doing?'

The boys immediately turned and ran in the opposite direction. She heard them pounding down the stairs.

The nanny came up to her, sighing. 'I hope they weren't bothering you,' she said apologetically. 'They see every attractive woman as a rival to their mother so they sound her out. It's a sort of compulsion with them, I'm afraid. You see, they lost their mother recently.'

'Yes. I understand,' Abby said. 'I didn't mind.'

'I'm Susan Reed, by the way,' the nanny said. 'I've been with them for three years, since before their mother had the accident. Do you know about Kaitlin?'

'Something of it. I saw her before she died.'

'If the boys didn't know I had a boyfriend, they would be giving me the third degree all the time, I expect.' Susan Reed tried to make light of it. 'One has to forgive them.'

'Was this…the family home?' Abby enquired.

'No. This house belonged to Dr Contini's parents—they let him have it shortly after the old man retired a few months ago. He was a doctor, too. It has always been a happy house so I understand.'

'It has a lovely atmosphere,' Abby agreed. The nanny had managed to convey that the former home had, perhaps, not been so happy.

'The boys were just sizing you up,' Susan Reed explained. 'When they meet you again they'll be more accepting. They're surprisingly perceptive when they meet women who are trying to cultivate them to get close to their father.'

It was difficult to make a reply to that so Abby was silent. She felt that the other woman was giving her a useful hint.

They heard Blake coming up the stairs, as well as a few other people.

'Blake.' Susan Reed addressed him. 'Do you mind if this young lady uses the phone in your room? The others are constantly in use.'

'No, of course not.' He smiled at them, and Abby's heart speeded up in anticipation of his closeness. After the slightly unsettling encounter with his sons, she felt once again that she must not get too deeply involved.

'Thanks,' she said to the nanny, and moved away, not wanting the perceptive woman to see the effect he had on her.

'Come this way,' Blake said.

The curtains were closed in his room and he switched on a bedside light which was beside the telephone on a little table. 'Take your time, Abby. I still have to say goodbye to a few more people. Some are still hanging around, waiting for the rain to stop.'

'Oh, Tim Barrick said he was going to be walking,' she recalled. 'Maybe he would like a ride.'

'He's already gone with someone else,' he said.

When Blake had gone she sat on the edge of the large bed, looking around the comfortable, spacious room which was furnished in dark oak, the fabrics in rich dark reds and greens, including the thick, patterned bedspread on which she sat.

Looking behind her at the mound where the pillows were, she tried to imagine Blake lying there. There was something very intimate about the room. If only it was something she could share…with him. During her teen years, marriage and motherhood had, for her, seemed to be something in the distant future because of her other obligations. Now she found herself longing for those things.

For God's sake! she admonished herself. Quit daydreaming and make that call! Her pager had indicated that the call had been from the locating service at the hospital.

'Dr Gibson,' someone at Locating answered her, 'there was a call from a Kyra Trenton—I think I've got the name right—one of your patients. She said it's not urgent. Would you call her?'

'Ah…yes.' Using a pen and pad that was on the table, she wrote down the telephone number.

It was over a week now since Kyra had undergone the operation to end her pregnancy. Her mother had been true to her word and had stayed with her, had supported her in every sense of the word and had not breathed a word to anyone. Probably they wanted to say goodbye. Kyra had exams to do before the end of term, then she would be going home with her mother for the summer holiday.

A wave of dizziness came over Abby as she sat on the yielding bed, thinking of the young girl—of how mature and brave she had been in her dilemma. Kyra was really Eliza Cruikshank's patient, yet it was to her, Abby, that Kyra had turned.

Closing her eyes, Abby fought the dizziness, regretting the several glasses of wine she had drunk when she had known she was very tired. She allowed herself to fall sideways onto the inviting mound of covered pillows. Just for a few minutes she would rest... She didn't think Blake would mind. Anyway, it would be a while before he was ready to take her home. She would like to sleep for a whole week.

On the window of the quiet room the rain was pounding, a soothing sound that made the charming room seem even more cosy and secure. After a moment, Abby swung her legs up onto the bed so that she was lying on her side, curled up. Just for a few minutes...

He must have been watching her for some time. When Abby opened her eyes she saw Blake sitting in a chair not far from the bed, his legs crossed comfortably, looking at her. His face was half in shadow so she could not fully see the expression on his face as she looked back at him through eyes that were blurred with sleep.

Oh, God! The thought came to her. I'm on his bed, sleeping... Maybe he thinks I did it deliberately. What an awful scenario if his sons had come in—their suspicions confirmed, perhaps.

'I'm awfully sorry,' she said thickly, having trouble getting her tongue around the words as she struggled to a sitting position. 'I didn't intend to fall asleep.' Distractedly she ran a hand through her hair, noting that her little straw hat was on the bed beside her.

When he got up to come and stand beside the bed his expression was veiled, yet there was a light in his eyes, a light of desire, that he could not disguise as he looked down at her. The shock of it cut off her hasty apology. Muzzy with sleep, Abby could only stare back at him as though mesmerized, her throat tight with an answering emotion, her heart rate speeding up so that the throbbing of it seemed to pound through her body.

'I'm so sorry,' she managed again, after a long moment when their eyes locked. Swinging her legs down to the floor, she stood up slowly. As she did so, her flimsy wool jacket that she had been holding slid to the floor. Simultaneously they both bent down to pick it up and their heads came together with an uncomfortable thud of bone on bone.

'Ouch!' Abby exclaimed, recoiling, letting him retrieve the jacket.

'There's an endearing gaucheness about you, Abby Gibson. A good thing you didn't choose surgery as a speciality,' he murmured as he straightened up, his eyebrows raised teasingly above his astute eyes that, although alight with amusement now, seemed to miss nothing about her.

'I'll have you know, Dr Contini,' she said, 'that when I did a rotation in surgery I was as cool as the proverbial cucumber—and not a bit gauche, as you rather unkindly put it.'

For a few moments they looked at each other, then, smiling slightly, he held the jacket open for her to slip her arms into the sleeves, while she registered that he was probably not going to respond to her mild rejoinder. That silence was unnerving. Turning sideways and then with her back to him, feeling absurdly conscious that they were alone in the secluded room, she allowed him to help her.

'Thank you,' she said, her voice a husky whisper.

Then his hands were on her shoulders as she had her back to him, easing her gently back against him. 'I don't mean to be unkind,' he said, his voice low.

Then his arms were around her, holding her... She felt that she could hardly breathe. For long moments they stood like that until she relaxed back against him, as though her whole body were sighing, finding its place at last, yet she made no sound. Instead, she closed her eyes, laying her head back against his shoulder. If I open my eyes, she thought, this will not be real...

His warmth pervaded her, his arms securing her so that she could feel him through the thin barrier of her dress.

More than anything, she wanted to turn so that she was facing him, so that she could put her arms around his neck, so that he could kiss her. Yet she felt paralyzed, the thought of his mouth on hers producing a lethargy she could not break out of…

Please kiss me… Silently she pleaded, almost dreading that he would break away from her when she so needed his closeness. Never before had she felt this intensity, not in any of her friendly, jokey relationships with her men friends. Cheryl had been right—she had treated them like brothers.

So this was passion, this helpless longing, this affinity, this rightness…this absolute giving in without embarrassment, this acquiescent waiting for the inevitable to happen.

As though he had listened to her thoughts, he turned her slowly towards him. Desire blazed in his face when he looked at her, taut with longing, his eyes dark. She had no doubt that her face was just as revealing before she closed her eyes and lifted her face to him for the kiss that she knew would come.

His warm lips moved over her mouth, tantalizing her briefly before he enveloped her in his arms, crushing her against him. With a groan of longing, he kissed her with a fierce, hungry passion. Instinctively Abby responded, giving herself with readiness, with certainty, while a rare, engulfing delight erased everything else from her mind.

Her arms, as though of their own volition, crept up around his neck. She found her fingers in his hair, then her hands holding his head so that he could be in no doubt that she wanted him close to her. Their bodies conformed to the curves and hollows of each other as though they belonged, the age-old belonging. There was no need to speak, and now Abby understood why as communication other than speech took over, sweeping them away into a mindless world of sensation and passion.

Somewhere else in the house a telephone rang. Blake, as

though awaking from a trance, pulled back from her. 'Abby...Abby.' He murmured her name, stroking tendrils of hair away from her face. 'What have you done to me? Hmm?'

When she did not answer, merely looking up at him, he moved languidly to pick up her hat from the bed to hand it to her.

'I'll drive you home,' he said softly. 'I'll bring the car to the front of the house. Wait five minutes, then come down to the front hall. There's a bathroom there...' he pointed to a door leading off his room '...if you need to tidy up. If my sons see us both leaving this room at the same time, they'll put two and two together and come up with a very high number.' With that, he gave another rueful smile and left her standing alone in the room.

Taking several deep, shuddering breaths, Abby tried to calm herself. This was what she had wanted, wasn't it? Interaction with a mature man? Blake Contini was everything that she had hoped for. No... He was more—much more—even though she forced herself to a sobering realization that while he was ready for a physical relationship, it was perhaps premature to hope that he was ready for emotional entanglements.

Her swollen and tingling lips attested to their mutual letting-go which had taken her by surprise. Devastated, she automatically went to the bathroom, locking the door behind her as though there were many prying eyes to witness her vulnerability.

Her flushed face stared back at her from the mirror, the pupils of her eyes large with her new awareness and... yes...her apprehension for the future. Falling in love with Blake Contini, if that was happening to her, would disrupt her life in ways that she could only begin to imagine. Also, getting seriously involved with him could cause problems at work, if only from vibes between them that other people would be aware of.

Emotionally he was raw, she sensed that, and very sensitive to the vulnerability of his sons. Having been a bad husband in his own estimation, he would not want to be a bad father as well. Although he had kissed her with hungry desperation, he had not done so, she knew instinctively, without an inward struggle. For a man like Blake, it would take more than a few weeks for him to get over the death of his wife, however he had felt about her in the end. She, Abby, could get hurt very badly.

They said little on the drive to her apartment building. A light rain still fell.

'Thank you for the ride,' Abby said, as they stopped opposite her home, scarcely able to meet his eyes. 'And...and I enjoyed the party.'

'I'm glad you came.' He smiled slightly, turning to her, unembarrassed. 'Tell me something...how well do you know Ronald Slater? You were talking to him at my house.'

'I hardly know him,' she said, surprised. 'I know him by reputation only.'

'I'm just jealous, Abby.' He smiled at her again, a slow, lazy smile that did strange things to her equilibrium.

'Don't tease,' she responded softly, feeling absurdly shy.

'I'm not. You're a lovely woman. He was looking at you as though he would like there to be something between you,' Blake said quietly.

'I can't help that,' she said. 'It's not reciprocated.'

Blake laughed. 'I'm glad.' He put his hand around her cheek and compelled her to face him. 'Abby...I want you all to myself.' Stifling any comment by putting his mouth on hers, he kissed her for a long time, gently, deeply, until he was the only reality in her world.

'Do you have a boyfriend...a lover?' he murmured as they broke apart and she lay against him, her head on his shoulder.

'Nothing serious.' Her voice came out in a husky whisper, as his fingers moved over the bare skin of her neck and down over her shoulder encased in the thin crêpe of the dress.

'Good. Now we know where we stand.'

'Do we?'

'Mmm, I think so. Thank you for coming today. Will you have dinner with me some time?'

'Well…yes. If you promise not to tease me too much,' she agreed, her heart singing with absurd happiness.

Reaching forward, he touched her lightly on the cheek. 'I'll be in touch when things are less hectic. Goodbye, Abby. No doubt we'll see each other next week.'

When the telephone rang later that evening Abby was in bed. She instantly remembered that she had not called Kyra Trenton. Although there had been no hurry to return the call, maybe she should have done so earlier in the day instead of deciding to leave it until tomorrow morning.

'Hello,' she answered carefully, the bedside telephone cradled against her head as she lay on her side.

'Hello, Abby.' It was Blake.

'Oh…I thought it would be a patient,' she said, feeling absurdly self-conscious, as though he could actually see her reclining in her bed, clad in the hip-length T-shirt she often wore at night. It was then that she had to acknowledge that she was missing him, that their shared kisses had breached a barrier that could not again be erected. A wave of warmth engulfed her.

'Are you expecting one? Not to visit you in person, I hope?' He was smiling, she could tell.

'No.' She smiled, too, a peculiar kind of happiness coming over her. 'A young girl—the one I was telling you about recently, in the cafeteria.' She told him what had happened in the case since they had spoken about it.

'I think you're handling it very well,' he said finally.

'Thank you,' she said. 'I…I don't suppose you called to tell me that, though, did you? Maybe you have another paper in mind that you want me to write—maybe for Monday?'

His spontaneous laugh eased the vestiges of tension between them. 'I actually called to say that you left your hat in my bathroom,' he said.

'I did?' Not surprising really, she thought; he had distracted her so much. 'That's my favorite hat—not that I've got many. It came from a thrift shop.'

'It makes you look…um…'

'Endearingly gauche?' She laughed.

'Just endearing.' There was a lightness in him, she sensed, that she wished she could see.

'I'll bring it to the hospital, or perhaps you'd like to pick it up some time,' he continued, his deep voice amused. 'As I said earlier, I'd like to take you out to dinner, Abby, if you'd let me. Maybe next week, Friday or Saturday? If you're not on call.'

Suddenly her throat felt tight with emotion. 'I would like that,' she managed to say. 'I'll pick up the hat then. Friday?'

'Yes. I'll talk to you next week. Goodnight, Abby.'

'Goodnight.'

Turning on her side and closing her eyes tightly, she pressed her hand against her mouth in a vain attempt to quell her churning emotions. Could she compete with the memory of the beautiful Kaitlin, if that was what she would be doing?

She felt as though she were going under, falling in love for the first time in her life. And she was far from ready.

CHAPTER TEN

IT WAS a typical June day, sunny and warm, promising to be very hot later, when Abby made her way to the hospital at seven o'clock in the morning on the following Monday. Dressed casually but neatly in a slim cotton skirt and sleeveless top, she delighted in the feel of the warm air on her limbs and the sense of being temporarily carefree. That feeling, she knew, would dissipate when she got to the hospital to start rounds of her patients who had been admitted, before she went on to a clinic in the family practice unit of the outpatient department.

The first call would be to Mr Barlow who was to be operated on that day. He was to have his chest opened up, a thoracotomy, to have a lobe of his right lung removed which contained the cancerous tumor. The CAT scan, the bronchoscopy and the needle biopsy of the tumor tissue had confirmed the diagnosis. As a patient, he was off her hands now as Dr Wharton, his GP, had referred him to a chest surgeon. The call she would make would be a courtesy call.

'Hi, Abby. How's tricks?' Cheryl met her going into the residents' change room. 'Super day, eh?'

'Too good to be in here all day,' Abby agreed, following her friend through the door. 'I seem to be running hard to stay in the same place these days. Not that I'm complaining. I'd rather have it that way when I have to be here instead of at a cottage beside a lake, basking in the sun.'

'Mmm. That's exactly what I hope to be doing next weekend at my parents' cottage... basking,' Cheryl said as she selected a scrub suit. 'I think I'll wear scrubs today as it promises to be one of those sweaty days. Want to come up to the cottage with me Friday night?'

'Well…normally I'd love to, but I've got a date Friday evening.'

'Have you now?' Cheryl looked alert, not asking any more questions as other people crowded into the room. 'Tell me about it later.'

'Mmm.'

When Abby looked at Mr Barlow's chart later on the chest surgery unit, having changed into a green suit and gone straight to the unit, she saw that he was to be first on the operating list.

'They'll be coming for him pretty soon for the operating room,' the staff RN on the unit informed her. 'The anesthetists like to have these chest patients down there really early to do all the preliminaries. I've just given him his pre-med shot, so if you want to have a few words with him, Dr Gibson, you'd better be quick.'

'I guess he'll be glad to get it over with early in the day.'

'Yes. He's booked for eight o'clock.'

'I see they did a mediastinoscopy at the same time they did the bronchoscopy,' Abby observed to the nurse as she flipped through the chart, looking at the lab reports. 'And the report came back negative.' A mediastinoscopy took biopsies of the lymph nodes from between the breastbone and the lungs to determine whether there was any spread of the cancer.

'Yes. Just as well for him, eh?' the nurse said succinctly. 'Maybe they wouldn't be doing the thoracotomy if it had come back positive. Wouldn't be much point. He's damn lucky, having smoked like a chimney for years and never had a chest X-ray.'

'I second that,' Abby agreed.

'He's lucky that all he has to have is a right lower lo-bectomy, that he doesn't need a whole lung out—or worse.'

'Yes,' Abby said. 'I'd better go to have a few words with him before he succumbs to those drugs you gave him.'

Gary Barlow had been in hospital for three days to have

intravenous vitamin therapy as he was not particularly healthy in a general way. The enforced rest and treatment showed on his face when Abby went into the small four-bedded ward where he lay ready to be taken to the operating room.

'Hello, Dr Gibson,' he said, more forthcoming than he was usually, lifting up his head to look at her. 'I guess this is zero hour, eh?'

'Yes. How are you?' She came to a halt beside the bed. 'I just came to wish you good luck. The pathology reports were very positive. No spread. So things are looking pretty good.'

'Yeah, they told me that,' he agreed quietly, fixing her with his pale, watery eyes. The sedative drugs were taking effect; he seemed relaxed and resigned. 'All I've got to do now is get through the operation...and the next few days. They told me I'll probably be in the intensive care unit for maybe two or three days, until the drainage tubes in my chest get taken out.'

'Yes, that's the usual routine,' Abby said reassuringly. What she could not tell him now was that he almost certainly had some heart disease from years of heavy smoking and, although he was a relatively young man, he was what could be described as an 'anesthetic risk'. The post-operative period would also be somewhat risky for him, too. However, she did not doubt that he would survive, and that he would get the best possible treatment from all concerned.

They continued to talk for a few more minutes until the door opened to reveal two porters and a stretcher to take him to the operating room.

'Good luck.' Abby smiled at him, squeezing his hand. 'We'll all be thinking about you in the clinic, and I'll be up to see you in the intensive care unit. Everything's going to be fine.'

'Thank you, Dr Gibson,' he said with dignity. 'I appreciate all that you've done for me.'

She stood back and waited to give him a final smile and wave before he was wheeled out. Tears were pricking her eyes. Most people, ordinary people from all walks of life, displayed that quiet dignity and courage in the face of fear and the knowledge of certain pain. They had to put their lives completely into the hands of others, and had no choice but to trust. As a witness to it every day, it never failed to move her. It was her duty as a doctor never to betray that trust.

With the familiar emotional lump in her throat, Abby walked away from the unit. Gary Barlow's courage reminded her of how Blake had been at the time of his wife's death. He had shown the same quiet dignity when told the news.

I love him. The thought came to her as she conjured up Blake's image while she stood waiting for an elevator and the bustle and noise of the hospital surrounded her. As though in a little island of her own, the realization came to her with absolute certainty. For better or worse, fate had taken a hand.

The elevator was crowded as she pushed her way in to go to another floor to do the rounds of her inpatients, before finally setting off for Outpatients. As she moved forward, holding her medical bag against her chest, she saw Blake at the back of the spacious elevator. They gave each other brief, acknowledging looks before she turned round to face the doors.

A flush of heat suffused her as she remembered his kisses, glad that he could not see her reddening cheeks. It was always a dilemma, getting a crush on someone at work—even more so falling in love with them, she was finding.

Willing herself to professional coolness, she concentrated on Gary Barlow and what would be happening to him now.

No doubt the anesthetist in the operating room would be talking to him, would be inserting another intravenous line. All the preparations for the operation would take time, the positioning on the operating table— A warm hand grasped her arm as the elevator emptied out on the ground floor, and she turned to find herself looking into Blake's eyes.

'Are you coming to the internal medicine rounds on Friday, Abby?' he said formally. 'We're reviewing Mr Simmons again, then we have two other very interesting cases, one of them being an unusual tuberculosis case. I shall expect you there.'

His eyes went quickly over her trim figure in the green scrub suit, over her slightly unruly coppery hair, her features. Abby found herself staring back at him. He was wearing an immaculate white lab coat over a formal shirt, tie and neatly creased dark grey trousers. His smooth, dark hair, cut short, added to his aura of sophistication and competence.

'Um…I'm planning to come,' Abby said.

'Are you getting out?' someone asked politely.

Hastily Abby and Blake moved out of the elevator.

'Good,' he said, smiling slightly. 'I trust you won't be late.'

With her cheeks tinged with colour, Abby looked back at him, knowing that her eyes were shining with an awareness of him. 'I'm usually very punctual,' she said.

'And don't forget I'm taking you to dinner in the evening,' he murmured, oblivious to people milling near them. 'I'll pick you up at seven.'

Abby nodded as he left her with a quick wave of his hand. How could she possibly have forgotten? She moved out into a main corridor, having forgotten momentarily where she had been going.

'Damn,' she muttered to herself. Life was going to be difficult if she could not speak to him without feeling like jelly inside, without feeling momentarily tongue-tied and gauche—even if endearingly so. She smiled, a little grimly, at the memory of his words.

There was half a year to go before she finished her training, then there were the exams, then she had to secure herself a job to get some experience. There had been no room in her plans for someone like Blake Contini. Anyway, men of his ilk were most likely out of her ballpark.

As she walked along briskly through the busy hospital corridors, swinging her medical bag, her heart was singing anyway. One day at a time, kid, she told herself, one day at a time. On Friday she would be with him, just the two of them.

She did not think for one moment that he was looking for another wife. A mistress, perhaps? Her feeling, like a certainty, told her that, if anything, it would be that...

Later, in the family practice clinic, her rounds completed, she called the number that had been left for her the day before from Kyra Trenton, getting Mrs Trenton on the line.

'Oh, Dr Gibson, it's good of you to call,' the woman said. 'We just wanted to let you know how grateful we are for all you've done for Kyra. Everything's fine now. I'm going to stay here with her in Gresham until she finishes the school term at the end of this month, then she'll come home with me. It has all turned out for the best.'

'I'm very glad to hear it, Mrs Trenton,' Abby said. 'If there's ever anything else I can do, you can contact me through the clinic here.'

'Will you be staying on at the hospital?'

'Well, I'm not sure. Most likely I will be, in some capacity, although I hope to be attached to a practice in the city—probably in the inner city,' Abby said. In truth, she was hoping to get a job, maybe, with one of the senior GPs with whom she now worked. If not, she would have to start out with one or two junior colleagues. In an inner city practice it was not likely that she would be meeting young girls from Kyra's privileged background.

'Well, good luck, Abby…if I may call you that. You deserve every success in your career. Kyra's sleeping now, but I'll tell her you called. Thank you again so much.'

It was gratifying to be thanked so profoundly on two occasions so early in the morning. Yet Mrs Trenton's questions had renewed her residual anxiety about the future, about what job she would get after her post-grad. finals. She hoped that Eliza Cruikshank would offer her a junior partnership—that was a promising possibility.

Resolutely, she pushed the thoughts from her mind and picked up the first case-history folder on top of the pile on her desk.

There were more people at the rounds run by the department of internal medicine on the Friday than there had been on the occasion when Abby had first met Blake. In fact, the small lecture theatre was crowded when Abby pushed her way through the door, carrying a Styrofoam cup of coffee that she had bought from the coffee-stand in the main lobby. It was exactly five weeks to the day since she had first set eyes on Blake Contini.

Making her way to the back of the room, she saw several of her colleagues there as usual, including Cheryl. The curious premonition she had experienced on that Friday five weeks ago came back to her—the feeling that the new doctor would come to mean something important in her life. Well, something was certainly happening…

Ensconced with her little group of friends and colleagues, she felt at home yet curiously elated and nervous. This was the evening she would be with Blake, just the two of them; the arrangement had taken on the air of unreality. She could not remember ever having had such a restless sense of anticipation before going out with a man, and she had certainly not been short of men friends.

'Hello, Abby Gibson.' A male voice addressed her and she turned to see Dr Stewart Hadley from Gresham General, dressed in casual street clothes.

'Oh…um…Stewart! Isn't it? You look different.' They shook hands.

'Right first time. You can call me anything except "Stew".'

'Have you come here just for the rounds?' Abby smiled at him, while Cheryl looked on, standing at her elbow.

'Yes. Dr Contini's fame as a teacher is spreading, it seems. He's got quite a reputation at Gresham General. A lot of our docs are making it a habit to come over here whenever he has rounds, and we're trying to get in on some of his clinics, too.'

'It's great to see you, Stewart,' she said sincerely. He was a very sweet guy, in spite of her muddled first impression of him.

'Likewise,' he said. 'I hope you haven't had any less than good repercussions over the Kaitlin Contini business? I understand that Blake was more cut up about it than the earlier indications would have suggested.' He spoke quietly, his head close to hers so that no one else in the chattering mass of humanity could hear what they were saying, except maybe Cheryl who seemed to be mesmerized by Stewart Hadley's expressive and somewhat charmingly boyish features, made prematurely mature by an overlay of chronic tiredness.

'It *was* very awkward for a while,' Abby admitted. 'And there still are vibes, if you know what I mean.'

'Yeah… That's inevitable, I would say. Believe me, Abby, it was better the way it happened. It had nothing to do with anything you did. It was her time to go.'

Cheryl's elbow nudged hers gently. 'Aren't you going to introduce me?' Cheryl muttered, scarcely moving her lips, her eyes alight with interest.

'Stewart, this is Cheryl, a friend of mine. I'm surprised you two haven't met.'

'Hi!' Stewart's face lit up as he took in Cheryl's pretty face at close quarters. 'Great to meet you. Are you in the family practice program too?'

'Yes…' Cheryl seemed to be equally smitten with the down-to-earth quiet charm of Dr Stewart Hadley as the two began to chat to each other.

Smiling, Abby turned to look across the expanse of the large room to the front where a screen was set up. Standing there, looking back at her, as though they were the only two in the packed room, was Blake. As their eyes locked his face held a bleakness she had only seen once before— when he had been told that his wife had just died. Abby's heart gave an unpleasant lurch of recognition. Perhaps it was the sight of Stewart that reminded him sharply of that day. Abruptly Blake turned away to begin the task at hand.

What am I getting myself into? she thought soberly, feeling oddly shocked. It was not too late to back out, she could cancel their date. But she didn't want to. No. She knew it was unthinkable—whatever the risk to herself.

The first presentation, given by Tim Barrick, was a follow-up of Mr Simmons. Blake took over when the younger doctor had finished, filling in some details about the case. Mr Simmons would be discharged home on the following Wednesday, June 24th. As was the usual protocol, he would spend four to six weeks at home, then would come back to hospital for a second course of chemotherapy—the first consolidation—and would be in for about four weeks. So far he was doing all right and there was cause for optimism.

At the end of the rounds Abby left the room with the bulk of the crowd. The expression on Blake's face had left her questioning any sort of involvement with him, yet she could not help herself.

Feeling unusually indecisive and emotional, she looked around for Cheryl, whom she badly needed to talk to. Her friend was engrossed in talking animatedly to Stewart, the two walking side by side, their heads bent close. They seemed to be getting along like the proverbial house on fire so Abby walked on.

The intercom in her apartment hallway buzzed that evening at exactly two minutes after seven o'clock, making Abby jump in her seat in the sitting room where she had been waiting, ready to go.

Chiding herself for being like a schoolgirl on her first date, nervous and jumpy, she forced herself to take her time walking over to answer it.

'Hello.'

'Ready to go, Abby?'

Rather than calming her with his arrival—she had thought he might change his mind—his deep voice sent her heart rate clamoring.

'Yes.' Her voice came out in a whisper.

'Great. See you in a few minutes, then.'

Abby dropped the receiver as she attempted to put it back on its rest. 'For God's sake, calm down! What's got into you?' she admonished herself fiercely. She grinned at herself ruefully as her inner dialogue came back with a vengeance.

Stalling for time, she went into the bathroom and splashed cold water on her heated face. It had been a very hot day, although not yet very humid as it would be in July, and the evening was pleasantly warm so that she could wear a simple sleeveless top and floaty, gauzy, short skirt that came to just above her knees. Even so, she felt that she was burning.

She drank some water, looking at her reflection in the mirror. She knew that she looked attractive. Her bare arms and legs had a slight honey-coloured glow from their exposure to the sun over the past two weeks, while the knitted cotton top clung seductively to her full, rounded breasts and the skirt which seemed to float around her completed the picture of summery youth. A little eye make-up and some lipstick added something positive to that picture, while her shining hair was loose and clung in wisps around her face.

'He'll be very aware that I'm a woman, if nothing else,' she muttered to her reflection, 'not just "the Brain".' With a reassuring smile at her reflection she left the bathroom and headed out of her apartment.

Like a lamb to the slaughter, she thought as she went down the three stories in the elevator.

Blake was standing outside in the evening sunlight, in the beautiful, burgeoning early summer that seemed so wonderful after the long winter. He was dressed in immaculate stone-coloured linen pants and a striped cotton shirt that, she could see as he turned towards her, was open casually at the neck. As she pushed through the double glass doors from the apartment lobby and walked towards him, he turned slowly to face her, taking in her appearance from head to foot with a casual, indolent assessment.

That walk seemed to take much longer than the few seconds she knew it did take, as his eyes lingered on her breasts, then on her bare legs as the hem of the gauzy skirt floated around her knees and exposed the lower part of her thighs in a way she had not intended. The sandals that she wore, with two inch heels, emphasized the length of her slim legs.

For the first time in her life Abby felt the potent power of her female attraction fully—she could see it reflected on his face. At the same time she felt her whole body respond powerfully to his physical presence.

'Hello. You look lovely,' he said softly, and Abby found her lips curving in a responding smile.

'Thank you,' she said. 'It's nice to see you out of a work context, Blake.' Even at his garden party they had been surrounded by people from work.

Leaning forward, with his cheek near hers and her

scented, newly washed hair brushing his face, he planted a
light kiss on her cheek, a gesture she now found both touching and spontaneous. Involuntarily she swayed towards
him, yet did not return the kiss.

Like an old-fashioned gentleman, he took her elbow and
helped her into his car which was parked at the kerb nearby.
Without making comment, Abby noted that it was a Ferrari
coupe and wondered what he'd done with the gray Buick.
As a car-less woman, she could not help but be impressed
by his good taste, in spite of herself.

'Where are we going?' she asked when he had settled
himself comfortably in the driver's seat, his long legs fitting
into the luxurious, tasteful interior as though the car had
been made just for him.

'A little bistro in a back street downtown,' he said, looking at her sideways. 'It's French.' Some of the tension she
had seen on his face earlier was gone, although close up
she could see that he looked tired, as though the months,
perhaps years, of strain had etched something into his face
for ever. Yet his sex appeal seemed to smolder just beneath
the surface of his sophisticated exterior.

'That sounds perfect,' she said lightly. 'I'm going to enjoy this.' As she wriggled down comfortably into the soft
leather seat which molded itself to the shape of her body,
he watched her for a few moments, then when her eyes met
his he looked ahead and started the car. The atmosphere
between them in the enclosed space seemed electric with a
new sexual awareness. Abby's glance strayed to his thighs
so close to her own.

Looking away hastily, she bit her lower lip hard and
stared out of the window. Before the evening was out she
would be in his arms—she knew that with a calm assur-
ance, as though it had been decreed. Too much work and
not enough play led to a certain amount of frustration, she
told herself, so that the letting go, when it came, was often
dramatic. She prayed that she could control herself enough

so that she would not do anything that was out of character for her. Being with Blake Contini was not going to be easy.

'I'm thinking of starting a journal club for the residents-in-training in my service, as well as the family practice trainees.' He started a conversation as he drove. 'Are you familiar with those?'

Abby cleared her throat and swallowed. 'For training purposes, where residents can present study papers and, hopefully, learn from them—right?'

'Mmm.'

'I went to a few when I was an intern, at the house of one of the staff men. It was great,' she enthused. 'He used to make it something of a social event as well.'

'That's part of the idea,' he said. 'Someone presents a paper, we discuss it, then we have a great meal and maybe a glass of wine or a beer.'

'The place I used to go to had great food—he used to get a caterer to do it, and we ate in his garden.'

'Did you learn anything, though?' he quizzed her, smiling at her enthusiasm.

'Oh, yes, a lot. I always maintain that a glass of wine aids the brain cells in the retention process. Where would you hold your sessions?'

'At my house. Would you like to come?'

'Yes…please.'

'I'm going to start planning it next week. The residents and I have already been talking about it. Maybe we'll have the first one in early July, if I can get one of them lined up to write something.'

'I shall look forward to it,' she said.

Thoughts of his charming home, with its terrace and lawns, came to her mind, as well as the knowledge that she would have opportunities to get to know him better, would perhaps meet his sons again, with their forthright nanny who would no doubt give away a few more of the family secrets, if one could call them that. The thoughts were oddly exciting, even as she chided herself for being presumptuous.

'It will give you a chance to meet my sons,' he said, verbalizing her thoughts. 'I'd like that.'

There seemed nothing more to add so Abby remained silent, basking in a warm frisson of pleasure at his comment and a small spark of hope for the future.

The restaurant proved to be as small and secluded as he had suggested, although obviously well known, as every table but theirs was occupied. The lights were low, the conversation animated, the ambience definitely French bistro. A table had been reserved for them in a corner, shaded by large potted plants. Under the small table for two, her knees brushed his.

'Sorry.' He smiled across at her. 'I'm afraid you can't sit here without touching. I hope you don't mind too much, Abby. I don't.'

When her cheeks flooded with colour he laughed and squeezed her hand as it lay on the table. 'Enjoy yourself,' he said softly, after the waiter had handed them each a very comprehensive menu. 'I think we both need that, don't you? The food is superb.'

With his warm knees touching hers, she studied the menu with an outward calm she did not feel. 'I think I need wine more than food,' she said, 'then maybe I won't be as aware of the unaccustomed knees pressing against mine. Do you think they do this deliberately with these tiny tables?'

'I expect so,' he said. 'Although I requested this table especially. It's the smallest in the place.'

When they both laughed, she knew that some of the tension would subside. Yes, she was going to enjoy this.

As time went by they both relaxed, finding that they appreciated each other's sense of humor. They talked about everything except the specifics of work, skirting most issues related to it, although they found themselves talking about medical ethics in a general way, philosophizing. They also did not talk about his wife, his marriage. With wine and good food they were able to laugh.

It was dark when they came out of the restaurant to walk to a main street where Blake had parked his car under a streetlamp. The warm air was like a touch of velvet. Wine sang in Abby's veins, making her happy and carefree. As they crossed the busier street he captured her hand in his and still held on to it when they had crossed.

Inside the car he turned to her. 'Would you invite me to your place for a cup of coffee? I won't stay long, as I'm leaving to drive up to my cottage on Lake Arbour tonight. It's a two and a half hour drive. I'm going for the weekend.'

'With your children?' she asked politely.

'No. They're coming for the next long holiday weekend. I'm going alone...to get away for a while.'

'Yes...it's a long drive.'

'This is the best time to go. Not too much traffic.'

'You're very welcome to have coffee at my place,' she said, forcing a lightness, trying to imagine how she would cope with his nearness in her tiny apartment. 'After that wine you need some caffeine to keep you awake. Have you got your bags packed?'

'Yes. I've just got to go home and pick them up.'

They drove in silence, the car seeming hardly to be in motion as it glided along. Abby knew that she would miss Blake over the weekend, just knowing that he was not in Gresham. It was irrational as he would not have been with her anyway. Now she wanted him to kiss her as he had in his bedroom at the garden party. She closed her eyes to blot out his presence.

CHAPTER ELEVEN

ONCE in her apartment, Abby occupied herself making coffee while Blake stood in front of a bookcase, looking at her books.

'Do you believe you can tell a lot about a person by their books?' she asked, standing in the doorway of the kitchen which looked out to the sitting room.

'Definitely,' he said, turning to look at her.

'So, what conclusion have you come to in my case?'

To her consternation he walked over to her, stopping just a few inches away and looking down at her. 'You are far more complex than you seem on first acquaintance, Abby Gibson,' he said. 'More so than you want others to believe.'

'Aren't we all?'

'No. Some are poseurs. Ultimately disappointing.'

'You mean they reveal all at one go, then don't have anything else to them?' She laughed.

'Something like that.' He returned her smile. A lot of his customary tension seemed to have gone out of him. 'I don't think you would be disappointing.'

When the coffee-maker made gurgling noises, signifying that the coffee was ready, she turned away.

Putting a hand on her arm, he detained her. 'Don't go, Abby,' he said quietly. 'Will you come up to the lake with me tonight to my cottage? You have the weekend off, don't you?'

Startled, Abby looked up at him, knowing that her eyes were wide and dark with surprise and an acute physical awareness. There was a sense of intense need in him. Not just a need for any woman, she sensed—he would be too discriminating for that. He wanted her, and it was a need

172

that she longed to put at ease. Yet at the same time the warning voices clamored in her brain as her heart thudded a response to him, to his magnetism, his attraction.

She lowered her eyes to his chest, where the opening in his shirt revealed the V of his neck. She wanted to lean forward to place her lips on his bare skin.

'I...don't know what to say, Blake,' she said, her voice little more than a whisper. 'Is that why you asked me out to dinner?'

He moved his hand up to her shoulder, his fingers touching her neck, caressing her. 'No...no, of course not. I just thought of it. I suddenly thought how good it would be if you could come. I know I should have given you more warning. Maybe you have other plans...?'

'I don't.'

Then there was a silence between them, a few moments of awkwardness. Perhaps if they had known each other longer, better, it would have been easier, Abby thought. Perhaps easier, too, if she had not been involved in his wife's death. But, then, the more you cared for someone, the less easy it was at first... She was definitely discovering that.

'Will you?' he said again quietly. There was no inflection of pressure in his voice, merely a simple question.

They both knew what it meant. He was asking her to be his lover. There was no way that it could be otherwise, in the intimate context of a lakeside cottage, just the two of them.

'Oh, Blake, I want to so much.' Abby breathed the words agonizedly, 'But I...don't know. I...wasn't expecting it, not now.' Bending her head so that he could not see her face, she knew that this was her testing time, the time when she finally grew up and took possession of that full womanhood she had been putting largely on hold. This was the time to say yes to the man she loved. But did he love her?

'No, of course you weren't...' The intensity of his need

was in his voice, in his hand, as he touched her. Abby
wanted nothing more than to surrender to that need, and to
the fierce urge that now clamored in her own body, making
the beating of her own heart sound like thunder in her
ears—yet she could not.

'It's all right,' he murmured, pulling her head against his
chest gently, his hand on the nape of her neck. 'I shouldn't
have asked.'

'Oh, Blake, I'm sorry...' With an impulsive gesture she
looked up at him and put her arms up around his neck,
giving way to her longing to feel his mouth on hers.

His eyes blazed down into hers, his face taut. All the
frustration and unhappiness that Abby sensed had been in
him over the past few years seemed to be in that look of
yearning. Although he was very attractive to women, she
sensed that he had not taken lovers during his marriage.

'You're the perfect treatment for me, Abby Gibson,' he
said huskily, 'and, at the risk of sounding pompous—
heaven forbid—I think I would be good for you. You've
had all work and not much play, I think.'

Accurately, he had divined her frustrations. For nights
she had lain awake, remembering his kisses, fantasizing
about him. Now here he was in the flesh, wanting her, and
she was stammering in agitation. 'Please, kiss me,' she said,
lifting up her face to his.

All the tension of waiting which had surrounded them
throughout the evening seemed to explode in the moment
that they came together, as his dark head came down to
hers, as his mouth captured hers. As she stood on tiptoe he
crushed her body against his, by enveloping her in his arms,
as though he never wanted to let her go.

'No... Don't go,' she murmured in protest when he
moved back from her, but then he was taking her hand,
leading her to the old, deep sofa that was in her sitting
room.

Without quite knowing how it happened, she was lying

on the sofa full length, her side against the back of it, and Blake was beside her. Simultaneously they reached for each other.

'I could die this way,' he murmured, his cheek against hers.

'Please, don't,' she said.

Abby must have slept for some time because when she opened her eyes again there was a thin blanket over her from her bed and Blake was gone. How could she have slept so soundly and not heard him go? A smell of coffee lingered in the air, coffee which had been kept hot too long. They had never got around to drinking it.

Slowly Abby swung her legs off the sofa. 'Blake!' she called tentatively, not really expecting him to answer. Her wristwatch told her that it was two o'clock in the morning.

Silently she padded into her bedroom to see if he had gone to sleep on her bed. No, he had definitely gone. He had, after all, told her that he intended to drive north to 'cottage country', the area of lakes that served Gresham as a vacation area. It was a long drive.

With an acute sense of loss, Abby wandered into the kitchen to turn off the coffee-maker. There was a note addressed to her tucked under a coffee-mug. Blake had obviously drunk a mug of coffee before leaving and had written her the note.

Hastily she scanned it, read the words that told her there were two trains on a Saturday going from Gresham up to Glen Arbour, the small town that was the closest to the lake where he had his cottage. There was a telephone number and a little map he had drawn of where he was in relation to the town. He would, he said, pick her up from the railway station…if she should change her mind about coming.

She went to sit on the sofa again to reread the note several times. 'Oh, Blake,' she murmured in the quiet room where she now felt bereft. 'I love you.' Wisely, he had withdrawn, leaving her to make the decision alone.

For a long time she sat there, thinking about her life and her work. Important decisions were never easy—at some point you had to make a decision and stand by it, not try to second-guess yourself all the time after it was made. That was what he had said, too.

If she went to him—and she wanted to—they would become lovers. Last night they had lain together, held each other, slept in each other's arms. Now they were ready for the next step. They could not go on the way they were. She didn't know what would come out of it, if anything. All she knew now was that she wanted to be with him, that she loved him, that he was a good man.

Thoughts of her patients tormented her also. Most of them had decisions, problems, that were so much more difficult than her own. At least young Kyra seemed all right, had her mother on her side. Ralph Simmons had a long way to go yet, with a treatment that was in some ways worse than the disease, yet he was holding up well. It made her own decision seem easy.

Gary Barlow was recovering well from his operation and there was hope for him, even though he was not a well man because of the negative choices he had made in his younger years. Then there was Will Ryles, made sick, no doubt, by severe stress at work, whose department might be taken over by somewhat shady private-enterprise medicine. There was hope for him, too; he was home now. Blake and other colleagues could help him...

Then, of course, there was Blake himself. A man of integrity did not easily get over the loss of someone he had once loved, even if that love had gone quite a long time before and been replaced by concern, regret and guilt. Then there were his sons, naturally loyal to the memory of their mother.

'So many loose ends,' Abby murmured aloud, 'and they

are not going to be tied up just yet, all neat and tidy. Not by me, anyway. I can only tie up some of them.'

Life wasn't like that—neat and tidy—least of all in the world of medicine. One could give optimism, foster hope and often give surety where there was hope. That was part of her skill.

'I will do my bit, to the best of my ability,' she vowed to the empty room. She understood that you had to do your best, know your limitations, foster hope in your patients and humility in yourself.

There was one other thing she could do…and she was going to do it.

The train took two hours to get up to cottage country, to the open fields, woods and lakes that characterized the region. As the suburbs, then the small towns here and there on the journey, had been left behind, Abby had felt her excitement grow to an almost unbearable degree. By the time the train began slowing down as it neared Glen Arbour, she began to rehearse what she would do, what she would say to him.

She had telephoned him from Gresham station that morning to say she was coming and he had said he would be there to meet her. Now it was midday, a hot, bright, cloudless summer day. She imagined him on the platform of the small-town station, waiting for her. It was a far cry from the hospital corridors, the lecture theatres, the bedside consultations.

Doors slammed all along the lengthy train after it had finally come to a halt and most of the passengers got off. There was one more stop for this train. Abby stepped down stiffly, hauling her overnight bag with her, scanning the people on the platform. Dressed casually in light jeans and a sleeveless blouse, she felt as though she were on holiday, light-hearted and carefree, yet she was nervous.

Making her way slowly to the station building, she could

not see Blake's tall figure anywhere. Pushing her hair away from her face, she put on her sunglasses and scanned the crowd ahead of her carefully again as she walked. A sick feeling of anxiety mingled with the excitement of her arrival. What if he had left a message at the station to say that he couldn't make it? Meaning that he had changed his mind, that she should take the train back when it reversed its journey in half an hour's time.

When she walked through the tiny station building she saw that he was not there. Other passengers went to the car park or got picked up by waiting relatives and friends, while Abby squinted around her, almost blinded by the bright sunlight.

'Abby.'

She spun round. 'Blake! Where…where were you? I thought you weren't going to come.' She blurted the words out, not bothering to hide her relief.

'Why wouldn't I come?' he said, smiling at her. He was casually dressed, already a little burnt by the sun. 'I was at the very end of the platform. Here I am.' His delight at seeing her dispelled any lingering doubts that he might have changed his mind. With that, he held his arms wide, inviting her to go into his embrace.

'Oh, Blake.' Abby dropped her bag on the ground, flung herself into his arms and gripped him tightly around his waist, feeling his taut muscles as he returned her embrace. 'It's so lovely here… I'm so glad I came.'

'Why wouldn't I come, Abby?' he repeated. 'Hmm? I've been waiting most of the night and half a day for you to come to me. *I* thought *you* might not come.'

'It wasn't a very difficult decision after all,' she murmured, her face against his chest. Happiness welled in her like a physical tide.

'Come on, let's get in the car.' With one arm around her shoulders, her bag in his other hand, they left the station.

On the outskirts of the small town that was little more

than a village, Blake took a narrow road that went to the edge of the lake and then continued along its shore. Everything was very rural, fresh and green. The scent of pine trees mingled with the scent of cut grass and country freshness, blowing through the open windows of the car as they moved along. Through the trees they could see the blue water of the lake, sparkling in the sunlight. After the muted colours of the city it all seemed brilliant, larger than life.

'It's so lovely!' Abby said again, gazing all round her at the changing vista.

'Wait till you see the cottage.'

After a few minutes, Blake turned the car into a gravel area at the edge of the lake and parked.

'Let's go down to the water.' He turned to her, smiling invitingly. 'There's a great view right across the lake from here. The cottage is around the other side, about a ten-minute drive.'

To Abby, he didn't look like a man who had been up for a good part of the night, driving through the darkness. There was a happiness about him she had not seen before, a mood that matched her own.

As they walked down to the edge of the water he took her hand, and she gripped his fingers in return, his touch like an electric current through her body. 'I want to talk to you, Abby…before we get to the cottage,' he said. 'Once we get there I may not be able to keep my hands off you.'

Abby laughed, walking easily beside him. 'At least I've been warned. I don't think I want you to keep your hands off me, Blake.'

Blake put his arm around her shoulders as they stood at the edge of the water, staring out over the lake. 'I shall keep you to that,' he teased as she rested her head against him and put her arm around his waist, an action that here seemed entirely natural now.

'Did I tell you,' he continued, 'that I bought this cottage a year ago?'

Abby nodded, understanding that he was letting her know that he had never been here with Kaitlin, that there would be no ghosts in this setting to come between them.

'I want you to know, Abby, that I appreciate you coming here. I wanted you to come so much, and I know it can't be easy for a young woman like you to take on a mixed-up guy like me who has been addicted to work. I've been no great shakes as a husband...' He spoke quietly, holding himself tense, as though she might suddenly take flight.

'I know what you've been,' she said, looking up at him. Was he telling her, she wondered, that he was prepared to be a husband again?

'I love you, Blake,' she went on. 'I know that's no panacea...but it's a start.'

Her voice was trembling as she spoke, betraying her hope that there could be something more for them than a year or two of weekends together of the passionate, abandoned love-making that would soon be initiated at the cottage on this beautiful lake. From her point of view, she knew there would be...for ever.

Apart from the mutual overwhelming physical need, there was a sense of something vital and wonderful between them, a sense of the future, fragile yet strong at the same time—like life itself.

The arm that was around her shoulders tightened, then he turned her to face him. 'Darling Abby... It's much more than I feel I deserve. I had given up hope of ever loving again, of daring to take a chance on someone who could love me,' he said.

His eyes, as blue as the sparkling lake, looked down at her with a tenderness that left Abby in no doubt that he loved her.

'I want to make sure that I don't go blundering into the same mistakes, that's all,' he said levelly, thoughtfully. 'I was young and brash then. Now I have no such excuse. I'm a father, the stakes are higher. You are very different from Kaitlin... You are what I need. Am I what you need, Abby? I want to be sure of that.'

'Oh, Blake...' she breathed, 'I love you.'

'What I'm trying to say is that I love you, too,' he said intensely. 'From the moment I saw you I knew there was going to be something for us. It bowled me over. Call it a premonition...'

'You did? I felt it, too, Blake!'

'I sensed that you did.'

'You can't go on feeling guilty for ever, Blake. We're both mature people, we've seen a lot of the world,' Abby said, her expression earnest, her heart singing with happiness. 'We're good for each other, I know it. You have to look forward, for the sake of your children.'

'Will you allow us the chance, then, to get to know each other better, my darling? For my children to get to know you? As I said, it's more than I had hoped for.' He cupped her face with his hand, tenderly so that she felt tears in her eyes—they were tears of happiness this time.

'Yes...yes, it's what I want more than anything. When I had the same feeling about you, Blake, that premonition,' she whispered, 'I thought I was being crazy.'

'No...not crazy.' When he brought his mouth down to hers to kiss her, she closed her eyes against the bright sun, his image in her mind.

The scent of pines was stronger here. Always she would associate that with him from now on, as well as the lapping of the water against the shore, the breeze ruffling the leaves above them, the sounds of birds. Then there was another sound, a faint sound like turtle doves.

'What's that sound, Blake?' she said when they pulled apart. 'Listen! Would that be doves calling to each other...courting perhaps?'

'It's the wrong time of the year for courting doves.' He

smiled down at her, his unguarded emotions letting her see his love. 'They've already mated, I think.'

'Oh.'

'It's probably the sound of unicorns, Abby Gibson,' he teased.

'You may be imagining things, Dr Contini.'

'Not this time,' he said, as he drew her closer into his arms. 'Not this time. This is once in a lifetime. My endearingly gauche Abby Gibson, will you marry me when you've finished your training—if not sooner?'

'Yes…yes. Sooner…please,' she said emphatically.

'Is that what you would prescribe for me—for both of us, Dr Gibson?'

'Definitely! Not only the perfect treatment—the cure, no less!' Abby laughed up at him, as the sound of wild doves—or whatever they were—echoed faintly, wistfully, around them.

On the other side of the lake the cottage waited for them. Soon they would start the beginning of the rest of their lives…together.

EPILOGUE

'Is THAT Mrs Contini?' Tim Barrick's mischievous voice assaulted Abby's ear loudly as she positioned the telephone receiver against it.

The telephone had been ringing all morning in the Contini rsidence as friends—mostly her friends—replied to her and Blake's invitation to the first barbecue of the year in their garden. She sat at a small, ornate desk in one of the sitting rooms in their home, overlooking the garden, where she had a guest list in front of her. It was a Saturday, with the relaxed warmth of early summer.

'You know darn well it is, Tim!' Abby laughed, happiness bubbling in her voice like something palpable. 'You're going to come, I hope?'

'Wouldn't miss it for the world, Abby. For one thing, I'm curious to see whether marriage to the former most eligible guy in University Hospital has spoiled your unreflective charm,' Tim said ponderously.

'That won't change, Tim—if you say I've got it! And let me reassure you that this barbecue really will be a simple nosh-up under a tree, with hamburgers on a smoky barbecue pit. We may even get you to cook them! It's a small group, informal in the extreme, mostly my friends, plus a few young kids,' she reassured him.

'You remembered!' He chuckled. 'See you next Friday evening, then, Abby.'

Still smiling, she ticked off Tim's name on the guest list, next to those of Cheryl Clinton and Stewart Hadley, aware that Blake had come into the room a few moments before.

'What won't change, my darling?' Blake came up behind

her, bending over her chair to plant a kiss on the side of her neck.

'That was Tim. He said something about my unreflective charm, whatever that means.' Abby smiled up at him.

These days they could not stop touching each other, holding, kissing, living intensely in the moment, their happiness so compelling that they constantly sought each other out, exchanged smiles, glances. They both knew how precious their discovery of each other had been.

'I want to make a date with you, Abby Gibson,' he said huskily, 'for a swim at, say, three o'clock prompt. Meet me in the cabana?'

'Of course,' she agreed.

'Susan's offered to take the boys to the air show that's on in Gresham. They've been bugging me to take them, but she wants to go with her fiancé and take the kids so I'm going to spend the time with you, Mrs Contini,' he said, squatting down so that he was at her level.

'Three o'clock, then.' she said, kissing him back, marvelling at how different he was now from the tense man he had been a year ago when they had first met. He was relaxed, his face reflecting the joy their marriage had brought him. In their own ways they had both been starved of love. Only with Blake did she feel intensely alive.

When he left the room she checked the guest list again absently, her whole body tingling from his touch. They had been married for six months…the most wonderful months of her life.

Winter had come and gone, and she had finished her medical training. Summer was beginning again, bringing with it all the promise of the season, all the promise of their future together. Later, when everyone else had gone out, they would meet by their garden pool, to be together in the quiet of their own shared place. True to his word, Blake was the loving, attentive husband that he had promised to be, never far away from her, while she was responding like the proverbial flower to the sun.

'Abby.' A small voice interrupted her contented reverie.

'Hello, Mark.' She turned to greet one of Blake's sons who stood in the doorway. 'Come in, darling. I've finished all my phone calls. Daddy tells me you're going to the air show with Susan and John.'

'Yep,' the boy said happily, advancing into the room. 'I want to ask you something.'

'OK.' Abby smiled, holding out an arm to him. 'Come over here. By the way, the six friends you and Jeremy invited to the barbecue are going to come.'

'Great! I…um…wanted to ask you something about that,' Mark said hesitantly.

'Sure. What is it, darling?' Abby drew Mark into the curve of her arm. Over the past months she had come to love the two boys, to appreciate the differences in their personalities, and was increasingly aware that they were accepting her more and more. She had not rushed anything, had taken her cues from them.

'For the barbecue,' Mark began, letting out his breath in a rush, 'Jeremy and I were wondering if we could call you Mummy. Um…Abby sounds a lot like Mummy so we might as well call you Mummy.'

The air of assumed nonchalance was so endearing that Abby smiled, kissing him on the forehead.

'Of course you can,' she said, her voice a little unsteady. 'I would be very happy if you would call me Mummy. If that's your decision, from both of you, then I'll accept it.'

'Yep, it is! See you later.' With that, he broke away from her and scampered out of the room.

Quickly Abby wiped away tears that had gathered in the corners of her eyes, tears of happiness and gratitude. Because she had been prepared for a difficult time with Blake's sons, she had been carefully non-interfering and neutral, helped in this by their nanny who had agreed to stay on for as long as necessary. Now her quiet strategy was coming to fruition.

Blake was already there when she entered the quiet, shaded cabana which had been erected as a spacious change room in the garden near the swimming pool. He reached for her, letting the fabric flap of the doorway fall closed behind her. There was no sound other than the twittering of birds. She and Blake had the whole place to themselves for the afternoon.

On Monday she would return to work, in partnership with Eliza Cruikshank. For now she would be nothing other than Mrs Contini…Blake's lover. Later she would tell him that Mark had asked to call her Mummy, then they would talk again of how soon they should have a baby of their own.

'Thank you, my darling, for more happiness than I dreamed possible,' Blake said,

They held each other, secure in their love. All their to-morrows held the promise of this moment.

MILLS & BOON®
MEDICAL ROMANCE™

VETS AT CROSS PURPOSES by Mary Bowring

Rose Deakin's job in David Langley's practice was hard because of her ex-fiancé, for David didn't employ couples. And he thought Rose still cared for Pete.

A MILLENNIUM MIRACLE by Josie Metcalfe
Bundles of Joy

Kara had a wonderful wedding present for Mac—she was pregnant! But her joy turned to fear when a car smash put Mac in a life-threatening coma...

A CHANGE OF HEART by Alison Roberts
Bachelor Doctors

Lisa Kennedy seemed immune to David James—how could he convince her that he would happily give up his bachelor ways for her?

HEAVEN SENT by Carol Wood

Locum Dr Matt Carrig evoked responses in widowed GP Dr Abbie Ashby she hadn't felt in a long time. Could she risk her heart, when Matt seemed intent on returning to Australia?

Available from 7th January 2000

MILLS & BOON®

MISTLETOE
Magic

Three favourite Enchanted™ authors
bring you romance at Christmas.

Three stories in one volume:

A Christmas Romance
BETTY NEELS

Outback Christmas
MARGARET WAY

Sarah's First Christmas
REBECCA WINTERS

Published 19th November 1999

FREE
2 BOOKS
AND A SURPRISE GIFT!

We would like to take this opportunity to thank you for reading this Mills & Boon® book by offering you the chance to take TWO more specially selected titles from the Medical Romance™ series absolutely FREE! We're also making this offer to introduce you to the benefits of the Reader Service™—

★ FREE home delivery   ★ FREE gifts and competitions
★ FREE monthly Newsletter   ★ Exclusive Reader Service discounts
★ Books available before they're in the shops

Accepting these FREE books and gift places you under no obligation to buy; you may cancel at any time, even after receiving your free shipment. Simply complete your details below and return the entire page to the address below. *You don't even need a stamp!*

YES! Please send me 2 free Medical Romance books and a surprise gift. I understand that unless you hear from me, I will receive 4 superb new titles every month for just £2.40 each, postage and packing free. I am under no obligation to purchase any books and may cancel my subscription at any time. The free books and gift will be mine to keep in any case.

M9EC

Ms/Mrs/Miss/Mr ....Initials ....
BLOCK CAPITALS PLEASE

Surname ....

Address ....

....

....Postcode ....

Send this whole page to:
UK: FREEPOST CN81, Croydon, CR9 3WZ
EIRE: PO Box 4546, Kilcock, County Kildare (stamp required)

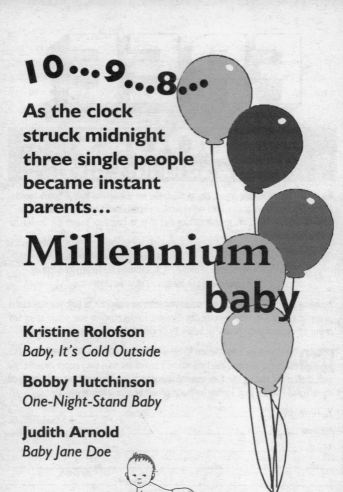